THE 8 MANSION MURDERS

SHINSOBAN 8 NO SATSUJIN

Paul Halter books from Locked Room International:
The Lord of Misrule (2010)
The Fourth Door (2011)
The Seven Wonders of Crime (2011)
The Demon of Dartmoor (2012)
The Seventh Hypothesis (2012)
The Tiger's Head (2013)
The Crimson Fog (2013)
(Publisher's Weekly Top Mystery 2013 List)
The Night of the Wolf (collection, 2013)
The Invisible Circle (2014)
The Picture from the Past (2014)
The Phantom Passage (2015)
Death Invites You (2016)
The Vampire Tree (2016)
(Publisher's Weekly Top Mystery 2016 List)
The Madman's Room (2017)

Other impossible crime novels from Locked Room International:
The Riddle of Monte Verita (Jean-Paul Torok) 2012
The Killing Needle (Henry Cauvin) 2014
The Derek Smith Omnibus (Derek Smith) 2014
(Washington Post Top Fiction Books 2014)
The House That Kills (Noel Vindry) 2015
The Decagon House Murders (Yukito Ayatsuji) 2015
(Publisher's Weekly Top Mystery 2015 List)
Hard Cheese (Ulf Durling) 2015
The Moai Island Puzzle (Alice Arisugawa) 2016
(Washington Post Summer Book List 2016)
The Howling Beast (Noel Vindry) 2016
Death in the Dark (Stacey Bishop) 2017
The Ginza Ghost (Keikichi Osaka) 2017
The Realm of the Impossible (anthology) 2017
Death in the House of Rain (Szu-Yen Lin) 2017
The Double Alibi (Noel Vindry) 2018

Visit our website at www.mylri.com or
www.lockedroominternational.com

THE 8 MANSION MURDERS

Takemaru Abiko

Introduction by Soji Shimada

Translated by Ho-Ling Wong

The 8 Mansion Murders

First published in Japan in 1989 by Kodansha Ltd., Tokyo
Publication rights for this English edition arranged through Kodansha Ltd., Tokyo

For information, contact: pugmire1@yahoo.com

FIRST AMERICAN EDITION
Library of Congress Cataloguing-in-Publication Data
Abiko, Takemaru
[*SHINSOBAN 8 NO SATSUJIN* English]
SHINSOBAN 8 NO SATSUJIN / Takemaru Abiko
Translated from the Japanese by Ho-Ling Wong

Contents

Introduction:
The 8 Mansion Murders
Sōji Shimada

The 8 Mansion Murders is the third *shin honkaku* mystery novel to be published by Locked Room International. I have been friends with John Pugmire, founder of LRI, for quite some time now, and the very first time we met—in his New York apartment near Riverside Park—we had a long chat, during which we discovered we had a shared interest in British open sport cars.

John used to speed along British roads in a Triumph, whereas most of my royalties were poured into my collection of MG's: MGA, MGB and Midget. Unlike John, my trips in those classic cars were made from Tōkyō to Kyōto, to meet with Yukito Ayatsuji, author of *The Decagon House Murders*, the first *shin honkaku* mystery novel published by LRI.

That was back in the eighties, when Ayatsuji was still a student at Kyōto University, and living in a room near Nijō Castle, where we would have talks about mystery fiction that often kept us up all night. His room was not particularly small, but it always felt cramped. Why? Because, almost every night, junior members of the Kyoto University Mystery Club would gather there to chat about new plot ideas for *honkaku* mystery stories and have lively discussions about the mystery genre in general. One of the students who was almost always there was Takemaru Abiko, the author of this book.

The light-hearted banter going on all the time in Ayatsuji's room was more like what you would expect to hear in comedians' dressing rooms. Other frequent visitors were Rintarō Norizuki, who would also become a celebrated mystery author, and Fuyumi Ono, who tended to join in the jokes from a safe place. She would later marry Ayatsuji and become a professional writer herself.

All the members of the group are now accomplished mystery authors, but if you had listened to them back then, you could have been forgiven for mistaking them for aspiring comedy writers. Never would you have imagined that they would make a career of writing mystery stories with an emphasis on logical reasoning.

Although I myself was already a professional author at the time, I was merely a listener, not because I held a position of seniority among them, but because their discussions were always so snappy and passionate that I could never get a word in edgeways!

Of the four, only Takemaru Abiko has made the joking they did back in those days part of his craft. Ayatsuji, Norizuki and Ono all considered the humorous banter purely as recreation, and in their own work they focus on serious writing. Abiko, however, is fond of his gags and jokes, and this can be felt throughout this debut novel *The 8 Mansion Murders*. His sense of comedy is reflected in the character of the young policeman Kinoshita. In a way, the Abiko of the Kyōto years is manifested in the person of the young detective.

Abiko's work can be incredibly varied and he can move smoothly between the various genre styles at will, from the *honkaku* mystery novel to comedy, science-fiction, adventure, psycho-suspense and human interest. This has made him an author with a dynamic range. Having known him for such a long time, I know this quality of his was developed in that room in Kyōto.

Through the snappy and amusing discussions they had, Abiko and Norizuki learned how to polish their plot ideas. Their attention to pacing would, for example, lead to new developments in their stories, or to the addition of new ideas.

Their relationship reminds me of how Clayton Rawson and John Dickson Carr's friendship led to the birth of new masterpieces. Having gifted partners with whom to exchange ideas undoubtedly widened the scope of their stories. I, on the other hand, was always writing silently and on my own, so I felt somewhat jealous of how much fun the Kyōto four had in the process of story creation.

It was during one of my stays in Kyōto that Ayatsuji asked me to read an early draft of *The Decagon House Murders*, which I would later help promote with my personal recommendation. Similarly, I would later write recommendations for Norizuki's debut work, *The Locked Classroom* (*Mippei Misshitsu*) and for Abiko's own debut. It wasn't long before I became known as the *doyen* of the *shin honkaku* movement which changed the world of Japanese mystery fiction. Be that as it may, what is certain is that the revival of the *honkaku* puzzle plot mystery story, in the tradition of S.S. Van Dine, started in Ayatsuji's room near Nijō Castle.

The three male mystery authors from Kyōto University would make their debut one after another: Ayatsuji in 1987, Norizuki in 1988, and finally Abiko in 1989. As I explained in the introduction to the English release of *The Decagon House Murders*, Ayatsuji and Norizuki managed to read the change in trends well and they decided to bring back the good old murder-mystery-in-a-mansion, building on the Van Dine tradition. At the time, the Seichō Matsumoto school of social realism dominated Japanese crime fiction, which meant Ayatsuji and Norizuki had no true rivals for their brand of the mystery genre, as a result of which their stories were seen as highly original. Thus did the student movement of *shin honkaku* mystery fiction gain momentum.

It was the emergence of this new trend that decided Takemaru Abiko to join the fray with a work in the same literary mould as Ayatsuji and Norizuki. Not only would that allow him to help the newly started revolution, it would also be likely to please an eventual publisher. Thus it was that Abiko, too, decided to stick closely to the Van Dine method, and make his debut novel a honkaku mansion mystery as well. As I was writing this introduction, I decided to ask Ayatsuji for his recollection, and he confirmed that he, too, had the same impression of the birth of *The 8 Mansion Murders*.

It was, however, Takemaru Abiko's talent that allowed him to handle such circumstances expertly. Ayatsuji and Norizuki had been able to write the stories they themselves had wanted to write freely, without any specific requests or orders from the publisher. Abiko, on the other hand, anticipated what the environment and the publishers would ask of him, and he responded by writing a murder mystery set in a mansion, and the logic needed to solve the mystery. His vivid imagination and wide, dynamic range allowed him to pull off the feat.

Because of its background, *The 8 Mansion Murders* is the perfect vehicle to identify what those students of the Kyoto University Mystery Club considered important in a mystery story, which they in turn derived from the writings of S.S. Van Dine, one of the most read and most influential mystery writers of the 1920s.

After reading an enormous number of books during a period of convalescence, Van Dine not only wrote several of his own, he also wrote twenty rules for writing detective fiction and suggested that the fair-play mystery in a closed-off world would be the most entertaining form of mystery fiction. While the authors of the respective works themselves deny the link, works published after Van Dine's peak, like

The Tragedy of Y and *The White Priory Murders* built on the views of Van Dine, and it was novels like these that opened the way for the Golden Age of detective fiction

The Van Dine method has been worshipped and widely used by many students belonging to Japanese university mystery clubs, most prominently those of Kyōto University. It is with this method that the *shin honkaku* movement managed to pave a way for itself in Japan, perhaps because, with its many set forms and rules, it fits well with the craftsman's spirit of the Japanese people. But another reason is that Van Dine's views and works also ushered in the Golden Age of detective fiction in the English-speaking world.

That explains why, more than sixty years after Van Dine, these Japanese students hoping for the return of *honkaku* mystery followed his methods and expertly crafted the framework so brilliantly used in *The 8 Mansion Murders.*

The story itself is solely about two murder mysteries and their solution and is almost exclusively confined to the mansion. It is as if the reader is seated in a theatre audience, looking at a stage which the actors almost never leave. The cast of characters is limited to the suspicious inhabitants of the house and the detectives. The murders occur under locked-room-esque circumstances. There are no untruthful statements in the narrative. The names of the various suspects and their backgrounds are presented to the reader early on. The detectives come from outside the mansion after the murder happens, but their deductions are all based on data already in the possession of the reader. And despite that, the detectives will arrive earlier at the truth than the reader. And the murderer of course turns out to be the person you suspected least.

Takemaru Abiko managed to create a story that perfectly fulfilled all those conditions, and he did it very swiftly in the short period right after Ayatsuji and Norizuki made their debuts as writers. It was as if he were an able student successfully passing the entrance exam of a prestigious university.

The story behind Abiko's debut novel throws a surprising light on the fact that as a literary genre, *honkaku* mystery has a unique plot structure. Usually, save for some rare examples, literature is born from the unique ideas a writer has in their mind, which they nurture and carefully develop until it grows out into a full-fledged story. This is the natural method for creating a story, but in *honkaku* mystery novels, the reverse is also possible.

The framework derived by the genre's pioneers from the Van Dine tradition can be likened to the exoskeleton of a crustacean: i.e. unchangeable. It is up to the *honkaku* mystery author to adhere to the structure, while expertly thinking of a story that goes inside the shell to give life to the crustacean. It is a delicate process that is not as much emotional as it is intellectual.

The circumstances surrounding Takemaru Abiko's debut also give us insight into a problem that is happening right now within the Japanese *honkaku* mystery scene. Ayatsuji and Norizuki wrote similar mystery novels for their respective debuts, but they were not craftsmen filling in a set form. Ayatsuji came up with a completely new method called "Symbolic Characterisation" as I laid out in the introduction to *The Decagon House Murders*, and also managed to brilliantly hide the identity of the murderer in his debut work. Abiko on the other hand utilised successful elements he borrowed from his predecessors in the genre. He used these elements like ready-to-use modules and by skilfully assembling them, he created his own story, as one would create a videogame.

The first murder of *The 8 Mansion Murders,* for example, is essentially based on a magic trick often employed in Europe in the eighteenth and nineteenth century. It was not invented by Takemaru Abiko himself, because one can trace its roots to magic tricks, but by combining the idea with the crossbow as a murder weapon—which on its own also feels like a familiar prop—he managed to give a familiar magic trick a completely new look. In essence, Abiko gave the ideal answer the teacher wanted to hear to a particularly difficult exam question, all within the limited time granted to him.

Currently, however, we see more and more works published by new authors all across Asia who look at the ideas from works of their predecessors as usable modules, and who freely implement those modules in great numbers in their own works. Their works do not seek to spring one single breath-taking surprise on the reader, but a whole series of surprises. Debates on this practice of modular usage have also started. Those writers who practice such an approach firmly believe that their own works become better with the adaptation of elements taken from previous masterpieces.

I will not dwell too long on the matter here, but I do want to point out that the notion of following the Van Dine method, following an approach that advocates working from the outside inwards, as practiced by many current authors in the *shin honkaku* movement, could eventually take us to a dangerous place.

Ayatsuji's *The Decagon House Murders* is in that regard an excellent example of a work that ostensibly appears to be following Van Dine, but which also features a completely original framework. Abiko's *The 8 Mansion Murders* is on its own also an impressive novel, but it might also have been an early sign of the shortage of new, original tricks in mystery fiction that we are now facing twenty years after its initial release. Having read it once again before writing this introduction, I realise now that perhaps the problem of the extensive use of module elements in mystery fiction might have its origins in the successful usage of the method in *The 8 Mansion Murders*.

Tōkyō, March 2018

Dramatis Personae

Kyōzō Hayami – Inspector of the Metropolitan Police Department, Division I.
Shinji Hayami – Kyōzō's younger brother.
Ichio Hayami – Kyōzō's younger sister.
Kinoshita – Kyōzō's subordinate.

Occupants of The 8 Mansion

Kikuo Hachisuka – President of Hachisuka Construction.
Tamiko Hachisuka – Kikuo's wife.
Kikuichirō Hachisuka – Kikuo's eldest son and vice-president of Hachisuka Construction.
Setsuko Hachisuka – Kikuichirō's wife.
Yukie Hachisuka – Kikuichirō's daughter.
Kikuji Hachisuka – Kikuo's second son.
Takao Yano – Servant in the Hachisuka household.
Yoshie Yano – Takao's wife, also in service of the Hachisuka household.
Yūsaku Yano – The servants' son.
Kazuo Saeki – Kikuichirō's secretary.
Mitsuko Kawamura – Teacher in sign language.

The western convention about names is used throughout: given name followed by family name.

The 8 Mansion (The Kikuo Hachisuka Residence)

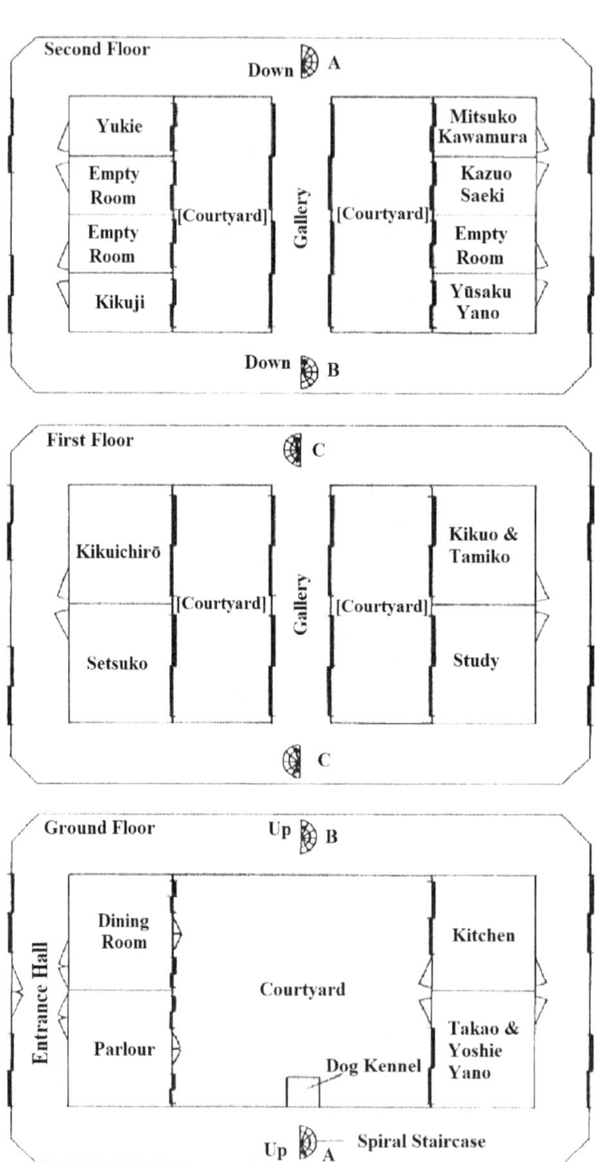

PROLOGUE

1

It does indeed seem to be an extraordinary plan.

Is it really necessary to go to all this trouble just to kill one person? It was a question I'd asked myself countless times. Couldn't I just sneak up on him when he was out on the street late at night and finish him off with a single stab from a knife? Couldn't I just push him off a rooftop and make it look like a suicide?

Of course I couldn't. That would have been meaningless.

To be honest, when I first started planning all of this, all I had on my mind was what I could do to get him out of my way, but now....

I glanced at the diagram laid out on my desk. It was the floorplan of the house where I was right now: The 8 Mansion. This bizarre mansion with its inner courtyard, designed without any consideration for efficient use of space or ease of living....

It was the layout of this very mansion that had given me the idea. No, perhaps I wasn't the first to consider it. The plan might have been waiting all this time for someone to find it. Just like the bottle of liquid that Alice found in Wonderland, it seemed to be saying: "USE ME."

It had to be destiny. This mansion had been prepared for me, so I could use it for murder. Or perhaps it was I who was being used by the mansion itself...?

But it wouldn't matter either way. All that remained was for me to execute my beautiful idea.

I did feel somewhat guilty for framing someone innocent for the murder, but he would no doubt understand my feelings if he knew how beautiful this piece of art was going to be.

Art! The "art of crime" is a loaded term I'd prefer not to use, but the crime I'm about to commit is definitely what one would call a work of art." Whether it would become genuine art would depend on my own skills... and fate.

The only regret I have is the absence of someone to admire and criticise my art – a great detective. However, I'm sadly aware that my hope for the presence of such a person is in vain in the Japan of today—in fact, anywhere in this world....

2

October 30th, Saturday. Ten minutes to one in the morning.

The home of Kikuo Hachisuka, president of Hachisuka Construction, is situated in a calm residential area in S Ward of Tōkyō. It was in one of the rooms of this building—commonly referred to as The 8 Mansion—that the telephone was ringing.

Kikuichirō Hachisuka, the son of the president, had just gone to bed, but even in his drowsy state he realised from the short ring tone that the call was coming from within the house, so he groped around until he found the receiver.

'Yes?'

There was the muffled voice of a woman on the other end of the line. Probably mother, thought Kikuichirō. 'Yes, it's me, Kikuichirō. Mother?'

'...There's something strange on the second floor. Come at once to the gallery.'

The female voice spoke rapidly, and hung up without giving him a chance to react.

'Hello? Hello?'

The contents of the call itself confirmed that it had been made from within the house. But by whom? Kikuichirō thought for a moment, the receiver clenched in his hand, but he concluded that the quickest way to find out was to go up to the second floor, so he slid slowly out of his bed and switched the light on.

Five minutes to one in the morning.

Kikuichirō's only daughter Yukie heard a knock on her door. She placed the book she had begun reading on the bed and got up to open the door. She knew who it would be. Mitsuko Kawamura was the only person who would visit her at this hour.

She opened the door to find Mitsuko there, as expected. In her left hand she was holding a small tray with two cups on it. The index finger of the other was initially was raised, but then she opened her hand wide and offered it to Yukie.

'I hope I'm not disturbing you.'

Mitsuko was using sign language. Even though it can't have gendered speech patterns as in the Japanese language, subtle differences in the movements of the hand can often betray the gender of the user. Mitsuko definitely "spoke" with a feminine touch.

Yukie shook her head slightly to indicate she had not been disturbed, and smilingly invited Mitsuko inside.

The latter placed the tray on the glass table, and her hands started to work busily.

'*I couldn't sleep, and I saw you were still awake too, so I poured us some cocoa. Will you have some too?*'

'*Of course.*'

Yukie pulled out a chair for her visitor, sat down on her own bed and took a sip of the hot cocoa.

Yukie had lost the use of her vocal cords about a year ago in an accident. It was then that she had become acquainted with Mitsuko Kawamura, who had subsequently moved into The 8 Mansion. She was not only teaching Yukie sign language and helping her with her rehabilitation, she had also become a much appreciated companion.

Yukie was a person with few acquaintances of her own, so Mitsuko had soon become an irreplaceable friend, someone she could rely on like an older sister.

'Oh, it's so hot!' Mitsuko had only taken a small single sip when she cried out. She stuck her tongue out, to emphasise how sensitive she was to hot food and drinks.

Mitsuko herself was neither deaf nor mute. She had originally wanted to become a nurse, but she'd become interested in sign language, and, almost before she knew it, had started doing work as an interpreter and teacher.

And to be precise, Yukie wasn't a deaf-mute herself either. There was nothing wrong with her faculties of hearing, so if ever she received artificial vocal cords or learnt to use oesophageal speech, she wouldn't be hindered in any aspect of her life.

But Yukie had no intention of getting artificial vocal cords and she wasn't putting much effort into her oesophageal speech lessons either. All the people living in the house had, up to an extent, learnt sign language especially for her, and as Yukie very rarely left the house on her own, she didn't feel the need to go through all that effort. But more than anything, Yukie was afraid that if she ever was able to speak normally again, Mitsuko Kawamura would have no reason to remain in the house.

Mitsuko's thick eyebrows shot up suddenly and the expression on her face turned to one of puzzlement.

'*What's the matter?*' asked Yukie.

'*I think there's someone in the gallery.*'

Mitsuko stood up as she explained with both hands. She went over to the window and opened the curtains slightly to peer outside.

'Oh, I think it's your father.' She had her back to Yukie as she spoke.

Yukie's father, Kikuichirō Hachisuka, always got up at six o'clock in the morning, whether he was going to work or not. Yukie could not remember a single occasion when her father had got up at this hour, however.

Yukie came over and Mitsuko moved aside to make room for her.

The fluorescent lights in the covered gallery were always switched off at midnight, leaving only the small red nightlights to illuminate the place. The figure standing in the weak light of the gallery did indeed appear to be Yukie's father Kikuichirō.

'How odd, at this hour,' whispered Mitsuko.

At that moment, Yukie noticed the presence of another figure and opened her mouth, but naturally no sound came out of it.

Yukie's room was located in the south-west corner of the 8-shaped house. The room at the diametrically opposite location, in the north-east corner of the 8, was that of Yūsaku Yano. Yukie could see a figure inside, standing close to the window.

'It looks as if Yūsaku is up as well. I guess everybody has trouble falling asle—.'

Mitsuko was midway through her sentence, when the two saw the figure slowly bring something up to its left shoulder. Kikuichirō, too, appeared to have sensed the presence of the other figure. He turned towards the north wall of the gallery, towards the open window there, as Yukie and Mitsuko looked on.

The following seconds would come back and haunt Yukie over and over again in her nightmares... in tormenting slow motion.

Kikuichirō's body suddenly flew up into the air, as if something had struck him. The whole scene was frozen in Yukie's mind as she watched.

Kikuichirō's body was floating almost horizontally in the air, illuminated by the red nightlights. Yukie felt as if she were witnessing a levitation trick.

In reality, of course, Kikuichirō had only been lifted off the ground for mere hundredths of a second. His body dropped to the carpet, bounced up once and then remained motionless.

There had been no cry, no noise of him falling to the floor. The only sound that had reached the ears of the two women was a wheezing noise, like the wind. Neither of them realised that the sound had come out of Yukie's throat, as she was unable to speak.

'*Dad!*'

She had been trying to call out to him.

'Wha—what just happened?' murmured Mitsuko in a trembling voice.

Kikuichirō was still twitching slightly. Something there was reflecting the red of the nightlight. Something metallic, something long and narrow, protruding from his chest.

When Kikuichirō had stopped moving completely, Yukie started to scream — a scream nobody could hear.

CHAPTER ONE: KYŌZŌ GOES TO WORK

1

'Inspector Hayami Kyōzō, you are hereby promoted to police superintendent following a special two-rank promotion,' the Superintendent General declared. His face was obscured for some reason.

'Did I hear you correctly, sir? A two-rank promotion?' Kyōzō asked in bewilderment.

'That is correct, Superintendent.'

'But what did I... I mean, it's a great honour, sir, but why did I get such a promotion?'

The Superintendent General looked back at him pensively.

'But surely you must know. A police officer who dies in the line of duty automatically receives a two-rank promotion posthumously. You were a truly outstanding police officer. You bravely confronted a brutal armed robber without any fear. Few could follow your example.'

'Sir, wait a minute! Wha—what did you just say? Died in the line of duty? Who did you say died in the line of duty?' asked Kyōzō in a panic. He sensed beads of perspiration covering his forehead.

The Superintendent General's face was still obscured, but Kyōzō could sense a pitying expression there, reminiscent of the Cheshire Cat.

'It's a real shame. Losing an excellent police officer like you is a great loss for us at the Metropolitan Police Department. Not only Division 1, but the entire Metropolitan Police Department is after your murderer. His capture is only a matter of time, so you can go to heaven without any worries.'

'To heaven.... Superintendent General! There must be some mistake here!'

Kyōzō's pleading, however, was interrupted by a sudden telephone call.

'That must be the telephone from heaven to welcome you. Answer it.'

The Superintendent General pointed to the telephone on the desk, which suddenly grew to a gigantic size, pushing Kyōzō against the wall. He tried to shield his ears from the ringing noise, which had grown louder in volume.

'Superintendent General! Help me! It's crushing me! The phone's killing me!'

'There's your two-rank promotion, Superintendent.' The Superintendent General's voice drowned out the ringing of the telephone.

'No! I'll do anything, even Traffic Control, as long as I get to live....!'

'Go to heaven.'

Ring, ring.

The telephone was indeed ringing. For a moment, Kyōzō feared his nightmare wasn't over, but when he realised he was now awake, he instinctively reached out for the receiver at his bedside.

'Yes? Hayami here.' He answered the phone just as he would on the police radio.

He had no idea what time it was because the shutters were closed. He fumbled around looking for his alarm clock. It wasn't quite seven in the morning.

'Inspector! We have a murder!' The excited voice of a young police detective could be heard.

'Is that you, Kinoshita?' He knew very well who it was, but still asked.

'Yes, sir! There's been a murder!'

'Yes, yes I heard you the first time. A murder, yes? But wait, what did you just say?'

'What? I said, there's been a murder....'

'No, before that. I think I heard you call me Inspector? Am I an inspector?'

'Huh? Well, you were until yesterday, at least ....'

And with that, Kyōzō finally had confirmation that he hadn't died in the line of duty. If he had, he'd already be a superintendent. But the fact he was still an inspector meant he hadn't. Perfect, cold logic.

A few days ago a police officer had been killed in the line of duty while chasing a wanted armed robber. That was probably the reason he'd had that dream. And while making it to senior police detective in Division 1 had been Kyōzō's lifelong wish, it also meant that, one day, he might suffer the same fate....

'Sir, is there something wrong?'

Kyōzō realised that Kinoshita had sensed he was still half asleep. His face turned red in the lonely darkness.

'No, it's nothing. Anyway, where is it?'

'Er, sir, perhaps you already know the place? It's called The 8 Mansion.'

The 8 Mansion was a curious building which, when viewed from the sky, looked exactly like the Arabic numeral 8. It had been the talk of the town for quite some time.

'Of course I've heard of it. It's pretty close, too. I even went to take a look at it when it was finished. And you say a murder happened there?'

'Yes. And it appears to be a very strange case. I'll give you the details when we meet. I'll be there by half-past seven.'

'Right.'

After replacing the receiver, Kyōzō revelled for a moment in the joy of being alive.

2

Kyōzō Hayami, 35 years old. Single. Height: 1.85 metres. Weight: 90 kilograms. Fifth dan in judo, third dan in karate. Passed the Police Inspector Examination recently. For his many exploits in Division 4 in the fight against organised crime, he was appointed to senior police detective of the Metropolitan Police Department, Criminal Investigation Division 1 (Homicide), Section 1.

His parents had died in a traffic accident ten years earlier and he'd taken care of his younger brother and sister all on his own since then. Taking care of his siblings is the reason he gives for still being unmarried, but that might not be the only reason.

He has nothing he would consider a hobby, but not a single day goes by without him practicing judo. His receding hairline has been a source of concern for him lately. His nickname used to be the Tank of Division 4, but as of late, that name had changed to the Bald Tank. Of course, now that he'd become a police inspector, nobody dared to address him like that any more.

October 30th, Saturday. Almost all the leaves of the trees lining the streets of S Ward had already fallen. Kyōzō arrived at exactly half-past seven at The 8 Mansion, the home of Kikuo Hachisuka, president of Hachisuka Construction. As soon as he got out of his car, his subordinate Kinoshita spotted him and came running.

'Good morning, sir.' The baby-faced police detective greeted the police inspector as the clear, cold wind coloured his cheeks. His suit didn't fit him, and he could easily have passed for a college student dressed up for his university entrance ceremony.

Kyōzō returned the greeting with a grunt. He always replied like that, whether it was morning or evening.

'Who was killed?' he asked, and Kinoshita took a bulky notebook out of his pocket.

'What's that notebook? Looks like a loose-leaf binder.'

'Have you never seen one of these before, sir? It's a personal organiser. One might even call it a miniature database. The future is tomorrow, and the criminal investigation of tomorrow needs to be conducted in a systematic manner. Look, it even has a calculator here.'

'Hmm, will that toy really be any good? Anyway, who's the victim?'

'Please wait a second.... You have these headers, you see. First you go to *Murder*. And the most recent entry is this one. Title: *The Hachisuka Residence Murder – Early Hours of October 30th.* I was the one who wrote this down just now of course.'

'And I am asking you who was killed! Can't you even remember the things you wrote yourself moments ago!?'

'Of course I remember. But I wanted to show how convenient this organiser is....'

Kyōzō sighed deeply and raised both his hands.

'Okay, okay, I give up. It's oh-so convenient. I'll get one myself too, I promise. But I beg of you, give me the name of the victim.'

Kinoshita returned to his organiser with a happy expression.

'I am glad you see how convenient this thing is. Let's see... The victim is the eldest son of the Hachisuka family: Kikuichirō Hachisuka, vice-president of Hachisuka Construction. The murder weapon appears to have been a crossbow.'

'A crossbow? Isn't that like a toy version of a traditional bow and arrow? But how...?'

'Please wait, I'm now looking it up under the heading: *Weapons*.'

Kinoshita started to page through his organiser again, but an irritated Kyōzō stopped him.

'Forget it! I'll get the details inside!'

The two made their way through the journalists and the neighbourhood housewives exchanging stories about whether it was a murder or a burglary, and ducked beneath the rope which had been placed in front of the gate to keep the public out. There was a sudden noise of camera shutters and several people started yelling questions loudly at them, but Kyōzō ignored them all.

The police officers of the S Police Station saluted the two detectives as soon as they saw the Division 1 badges Kyōzō and Kinoshita were sporting on their suits.

Kyōzō was first through the gate, and stopped to glance up at the building. It was an ordinary three-storey building made out of reinforced concrete. It didn't look to him like a home so much as a fancy office building. When viewed from the sky—Kyōzō himself had only seen it on television—the building looked like the Arabic numeral 8 because of what appeared to be two inner courtyards in the middle of the house.

The master of the house, Kikuo Hachisuka, was rumoured to be quite an eccentric type. Partly as a way to promote his own construction company, he had first planned to build his house in the form of a bee—the *hachi* in Hachisuka meant "bee"—but had been forced to give up the idea for various reasons, including protests from his own family and problems surrounding the design and liveability of the place, and in the end he'd gone with the 8 design. While written differently, the numeral 8 is also pronounced *hachi* in Japanese, so Kikuo had decided to settle for wordplay. A television commercial themed after a bee's 8-figured waggle dance showed the mansion from above. The slogan was "Hachisuka Construction Can Build Anything," and it had been chosen as the worst commercial last year.

But while it was not clear whether the promotion surrounding the house had actually helped, Hachisuka Construction share prices had risen and rumours said it would become a listed share soon. In the construction world, people started to call Kikuo the Adventurer of the Construction Industry.

That was basically all Kyōzō knew about the building.

When the two detectives arrived at the front door, it was opened for them by a police officer. The entrance hall was located at the centre of the south side of the 8. The doors to the room across from the entrance—probably the parlour—were open and a large number of people were milling around inside.

'Welcome, Inspector.'

The first to notice their arrival was Detective Sergeant Okuda of S Police Station. Kyōzō had never worked with him before on a case, but they had been opponents several times at judo tournaments.

Kyōzō himself was tall and heavily-built, but Okuda was twenty kilograms heavier and several centimetres taller. Kyōzō had been up against him in the open-weight tournament semi-finals earlier in the year and had sadly lost on points.

'Oh, it's you.' Kyōzō did not try to cover up his displeasure. His aversion to Okuda was something physiological. The man's bad breath was one of the reasons, and Kyōzō was convinced that was the only reason he had lost.

'Must have been a long trip from Sakuradamon all the way down here,' Okuda said with a mocking tone as he spewed out a cloud of bad breath[i].

Kyōzō turned his face away from Okuda and stepped inside the room. The parlour was more than thirty square meters in area, the floor covered by an emerald deep pile carpet on which stood modern, round designer sofas. On the north side of the room, opposite the entrance doors, were French windows leading to an inner courtyard covered by a beautiful grass lawn; a gigantic St. Bernard, tied to a dog house on the lawn, gazed sadly towards the parlour.

Seven people were seated on the sofas. Behind the old gentleman who appeared to be the master of the house stood a man who was no doubt his secretary. A man and a woman, probably the servants, were standing in one corner of the room, watching all that happened with restless eyes.

'I'm Police Inspector Hayami of the Homicide Division,' announced Kyōzō. 'I'll be handling this case together with Detective-Sergeant Okuda of the S Police Station. This is my subordinate, Kinoshita. Thank you for your cooperation.'

He bowed his head deeply, and several people returned the greeting.

Okuda proceeded to make the introductions.

'The person sitting there in the back is Mr. Kikuo. And sitting on his left side is Tamiko, his wife. To his right is his younger son, Kikuji. And the two standing over there are the servants, the Yanos. And the woman who is er... comforting herself with some spirits is the dea—I mean the victim's wife, Setsuko.'

Okuda fell silent for a moment, perhaps debating whether attempting to down a whole bottle of spirits qualified as "comforting herself."

'And on this sofa, we have the Yanos's son, Yūsaku, Kikuichirō's daughter, Yukie, and Ms. Mitsuko Kawamura, who teaches Yukie sign language. Oh, I almost forgot. The man standing behind Mr.

Kikuo is the victim's secretary, Mr. Kazuo Saeki, who also lives here in the house.'

Kyōzō silently nodded to everyone as he memorised their faces and names, whilst Kinoshita scribbled busily in his organiser.

Okuda took a deep breath and continued: 'Now I'd like to go over everyone's statements again. Let's start with the person who discovered the crime, Ms. Mitsuko Kawamura. It was you who notified the police, is that correct?'

The woman he addressed was cute enough, even though her clothes were drab. She was very small—maybe not even 1.50 meters tall—and her delicate build made her look almost like a child, although she was probably in her mid-twenties.

Kyōzō wondered about the bandages wrapped around her head. The woman sitting next to her with downcast eyes also had her head bandaged.

'Yes, I called the police.'

'Could you please repeat your statement once again, from the beginning?'

Mitsuko shot a glance at the woman sitting next to her before she started to speak.

'I was together with Yukie in her room, and we were still up, even though it was late. I think it was at about one o'clock in the morning when we saw someone walking down the covered gallery —that's the connecting corridor above the inner courtyard. It corresponds to the centre line of the 8-shape of this house. We knew right away it was Mr. Kikuichirō. He appeared to be looking for someone. We thought it was odd, because everybody in this house goes to bed early, so we kept looking, and then....'

The woman sitting next to her trembled suddenly and started to sob silently. Mitsuko gently placed a hand on top of hers.

'Mr. Kikuichirō suddenly turned his head to look at a room on the other side of where we were. There was somebody there. But the lights were out, so I could only make out vague shapes. At that moment I saw something projecting from the room. Suddenly Mr. Kikuichirō grabbed at his chest and collapsed. From where we stood, we could clearly see something sticking out from his chest as he lay on the floor.'

Okuda turned to Kyōzō and whispered something in his ear: 'It was a crossbow. The servants' son, Yūsaku Yano—sitting over there—owns a crossbow, but he says he lost it a while ago. It's supposed to be very powerful. Appears the arrow broke some ribs and pierced the heart.'

Mitsuko waited for Okuda to turn his attention to her again, then continued. 'I went out of the room to see what had happened to Mr. Kikuichirō. But I was halfway along the hallway when someone struck me, and I was knocked out.'

'Did you catch a glimpse of your assailant? For example, whether it was a man or a woman?' interjected Kyōzō, but Mitsuko shook her head apologetically. Perhaps her head hurt, because her face was contorted.

'And that's why your call to the police was delayed.'

'Yes.'

'Now then, what were you doing all this time, Miss Yukie?'

The woman next on Okuda's list was sitting next to Mitsuko. Yukie gently wiped away her tears and looked up.

Kyōzō felt his heart stop. This woman was gorgeous. Her skin was deathly pale and her eyes were red and swollen from crying, but, despite all that, she was beautiful.

So pure and so neat.

The image of a woman playing the violin in a white villa surrounded by a forest flashed through Kyōzō's mind. She was, of course, wearing a pure white dress.

Kyōzō had been dreaming of such a divine creature since middle school. She was his ideal woman.

While he was staring dreamily at her, Yukie turned to Mitsuko and started to make strange motions with her hands. Kyōzō immediately realised she was using sign language.

Kyōzō turned to Okuda in surprise.

'Yukie Hachisuka can't speak,' said his colleague.

'Can't she talk at all?'

'No. She was in a traffic accident about a year ago, and they had to remove her vocal cords, or so I hear.'

When Yukie had ended her sign language message, Mitsuko continued her account.

'After I'd left the room, Yukie became worried because I was taking so long to return. She waited for about three minutes and then stepped out of the room herself, but was immediately attacked by someone who'd been hiding behind the door. She lost consciousness, just like me.'

Yukie nodded several times as she listened to Mitsuko's interpretation. She was still able to hear.

'Who recovered first?' asked Okuda, and Yukie raised her hand.

'Yukie woke me up,' said Mitsuko. 'Then the two of us went to see what had happened to Mr. Kikuichirō, but by that time....'

She shook her head ruefully.

'... he'd already passed away.'

'According to the police surgeon, he died instantly and felt no pain,' Okuda reassured the two women. He turned back to Kyōzō.

'So now you've a pretty good idea of what happened, all right?'

'Enough for now. By the way, have you found the weapon?'

'We have the arrow, obviously, but I'm afraid we haven't found the crossbow itself yet,' replied Okuda.

'Where's the room they say the murderer was standing in?'

'I'll show you right away.'

3

Kyōzō and Kinoshita followed Okuda's lead. In the west wing of the 8 stood a spiral staircase, and they used that to go up two flights of stairs.

'This is where the corpse was found,' explained Okuda when they arrived on the second floor, pointing towards the covered gallery. From a bird's eye view, the galleries on the first and second floor divided the single inner courtyard on the ground floor into two visually, giving the building its distinctive 8 design.

Near the centre of the gallery, on the west half of the red carpet, a piece of white rope had been placed, arranged in the shape of a human figure. A bored-looking police officer was standing guard there, but as soon as he saw the three men come up, he quickly corrected his posture and saluted.

Kyōzō waved his hand to the man, approached the rope and bent down to examine the shape.

'Something curious here, though. Somebody moved the body,' said Okuda from behind him.

'You mean he didn't die here? But didn't those two women see the murder happen?' asked Kyōzō, frowning.

'Well, when I say moved, I mean his body was dragged down this carpet a short way. If you look over here you'll notice a few spots of blood.'

Diagram 1: How The Body Was Discovered

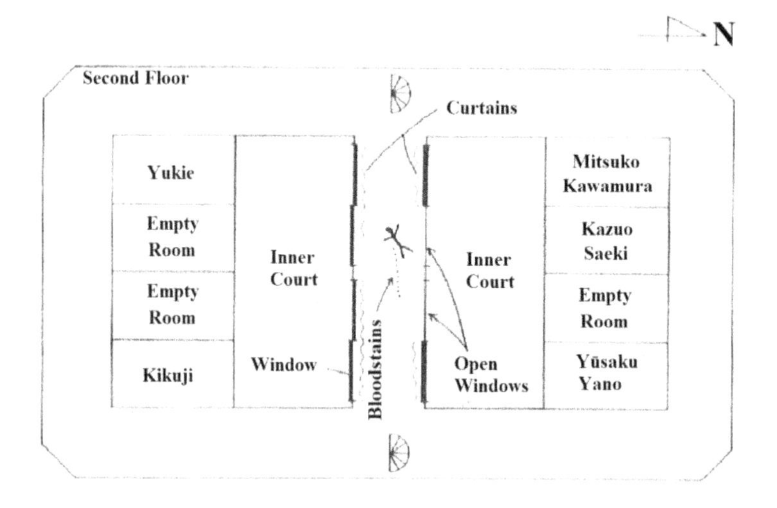

As Okuda had pointed out, there were indeed a few drops of blood here and there, trailing from the white outline of the body across the carpet towards the east. The trail was about two metres long and stopped abruptly.

'I see. That means the body was lying east of the centre at first, but was then dragged slightly west by the killer. And what did the witnesses say? Where did the victim fall?'

'They both say he fell east of the centre. The culprit probably tried to move the body somewhere else, but then gave up for some reason.'

'Was the victim large?'

'No, he weighed about sixty kilograms—in other words, about average. Even a woman could've dragged him along the floor. Whoever the killer may be, I don't think they gave up on the idea just because of the weight.'

Kyōzō went over to the place where the body had probably fallen originally and looked around.

'That's Yukie's room over there. And almost diagonally opposite is the room where they say the murderer was.'

Okuda went over to Kyōzō's side, and pointed towards to the second room of the northern wing, counted from the east. (See diagram 1)

'I don't believe anything of that story, mind you,' Okuda added with a grin.

'What do you mean?'

'You'll know when you've seen it for yourself.'

Okuda walked along the gallery and led Kyōzō to the room in question. He took a bundle of keys from his pocket and used one of them to open the door.

'This is one of the guest rooms, and is not in use at the moment. It had been kept locked for the last few months. There are two keys to the room, but both are kept together on this bundle, which is taken care of by Takao Yano, one of the servants here.'

The room reminded Kyōzō of a hotel room. It was about fourteen square metres in area, and contained a bed, a small table, two chairs, and a closet set against the wall. The window was right opposite the door. On the other side of the window, crossing over the inner courtyard, was the covered gallery they had stood on moments ago.

'The window is also kept locked.'

'So what you mean is that nobody could have entered this room save for this Takao Yano?'

'Precisely.'

'And there are no other spare keys?'

'Unless he himself had one made in secret, nobody would even have had the chance to make a spare.'

Kyōzō exclaimed, in surprise: 'But that means this Takao is our man! It's clear as day!'

'It is not as simple as that, my dear Inspector, for Takao Yano appears to possess an iron-clad alibi,' said Okuda mockingly. With a small cry, Kinoshita opened his organiser and started creating a header for *Alibis*. Kyōzō ignored him and asked:

'So nobody could have entered this room? You mean, it's one of those... locked room mysteries?'

'It appears so.'

'Couldn't you just open the door with a plastic card or a hairpin?'

The locks in houses like these could often be opened simply by inserting a plastic card in the gap between the door and the frame. Kyōzō was thinking of that possibility as he crouched down to examine the lock.

'We already checked for that. It's a fine lock. There's no way that trick would've worked,' said Okuda sneeringly as he rejected the idea.

Kyōzō grunted and reflected for a while, then asked:

'So what's your conclusion?'

'Those two witnesses were lying, obviously. The Kawamura woman is pretty shrewd, and I almost believed her, but the Yukie woman was obviously acting strangely. Those two are hiding something, no doubt about it.'

Kyōzō was getting annoyed with Okuda. He was offended for two reasons: first because Okuda had referred to Yukie as "the Yukie woman" and secondly because he had called her a liar.

'But she didn't appear to be a liar to me. Are you sure there aren't any secret passageways here?'

'This house was designed by the old man, and he showed us the plans. No secret passageways. We did knock on the walls just to be sure. But this is obviously not a ninja castle with dozens of hiding spots and secret hallways....'

'Those two women might have simply been mistaken about what they witnessed. Have you looked into that?'

'Of course, but they are both sure it was this room.'

'Hmm. So what's your next step?'

'What's the next step a police inspector of Division 1 would take?' Okuda returned the question with a faint grin on his face.

It was only then that Kyōzō realised that Okuda wasn't all that fond of him either. Okuda was probably just jealous of the title of Police Inspector of the Metropolitan Police Department. His attitude was certainly not pleasant.

I can't afford to make any mistakes here, Kyōzō thought to himself.

'We need to question both Mitsuko Kawamura and Yukie separately,' he announced. 'Kinoshita, call Mitsuko Kawamura up here.'

Kinoshita was still absorbed in designing the *Alibis* header, using refill planner pages to write down the movements of all the suspects.

'Kinoshita! Didn't you hear my order?!'

Kinoshita jumped up abruptly, dropping his refill pages all over the floor.

'Oh no, I had them all sorted out....'

'Forget about that and get to work!'

Kyōzō bared his teeth as he glared at Kinoshita, who flew out of the room.

4

Kyōzō and Mitsuko sat across from each other, separated by the small table.

'Ms. Kawamura, according to Ms.Yukie and your own statement, Mr. Kikuichirō was shot by the murderer from this room. Are you absolutely sure about that?'

'Yes,' Mitsuko replied without any sign of hesitation.

'But at the time of the crime, the door and the window of this room were all locked. It would've been impossible for anyone to enter.'

Mitsuko cocked her head to one side.

'But Mr. Yano should have the key... Oh, of course I don't mean to imply that he committed the crime....'

Okuda leant forward and interjected: 'But Mr. Yano wasn't here in the house at the time of the crime. He'd gone out for drinks. And taken his bundle of keys with him.'

At those words, Mitsuko suddenly turned pale.

'...And that's why Okuda here has concluded that you two have been telling us a lie. If he's right, I want you to tell us the truth now. You are aware that making a false testimony is a crime, I assume?' said Kyōzō, applying pressure.

Mitsuko looked down in silence. Years of experience told Kyōzō that she was now preparing to tell the truth.

She looked up and started speaking in an apologetic manner: 'I'm terribly sorry. Actually, we didn't see the murderer in this room. But neither Yukie nor I could believe that he would do such a thing....'

'So your statement was a complete fabrication?'

Kyōzō felt a slight disappointment learning that Okuda had been right.

'No, we only indicated the wrong room. The rest is all true.'

'I see. And who is this "he" you mentioned?'

Mitsuko bit on her lip for a while, but then answered the question.

'Yūsaku Yano. Mr. Yano's son.'

'So you saw the murderer in Yūsaku's room? Did you recognise him?'

'No, it was too dark! I still can't believe that Yūsaku would have killed Mr. Kikuichirō! That is why Yukie and I talked it over, and decided to say the murderer was in a different room.'

'And where's Yūsaku's room?'

'It's the one right next door,' said Mitsuko, bowing her head.

Kyōzō sent Mitsuko away and called for Yukie. He'd feared he would need to ask her to write down her answers, but to his surprise, she had brought a small word processor with her. It was about as big as a notebook, but there was no printer attached to it.

As soon as she sat down, she opened the word processor on her lap and placed her delicate fingers on the keyboard, awaiting Kyōzō's questions.

Kyōzō decided to be straightforward.

'Miss Yukie, Ms. Mitsuko has just admitted to us that you lied in your statements. She said the two of you had talked it over.'

Yukie was visibly surprised.

She started to type with trembling fingers. Letters started to appear one after another on the small display.

'*He didn't do it. There is no way he'd have killed dad.*'

'I assume you're talking about Yūsaku Yano?'

Yukie looked pained as she bit her lip, but nodded.

'So you didn't see the murderer in this room, but in Yūsaku's room, the room next door?'

'*Yes. But he didn't do it.*'

'And why do you think that?'

'*He's not like that. He didn't have any reason to do it.*'

'We'll have to ask him ourselves about that. I gather that you couldn't make out who the murderer was because of the darkness. So it might have been Yūsaku, is that correct?'

Yukie stopped using her word processor and just sat looking down at the floor.

'Thank you. You can leave now.'

Kyōzō wanted to say something to her—anything—as she stood up listlessly and left the room, but he couldn't find the right words.

'Kinoshita, get me Yūsaku Yano.'

Kinoshita had finally finished the category *Alibis*, so he responded with alacrity this time.

Yūsaku came into the room, wearing a docile expression. He had clearly no inkling that he was a suspect. He was well-built, with the body of a sportsman.

'You are Yūsaku Yano?'

'Yes.'

'University student?'

'Yes. I'm in my fourth year.'

He seemed a bit nervous, but that was perhaps quite natural, being faced with the two giants Kyōzō and Okuda. He seemed like an earnest individual and Kyōzō couldn't imagine he would have anything suspicious to hide.

'The crossbow thought to be the murder weapon is yours, is that correct?'

'Yes. It went missing about a week ago. Given what's happened, I assume the murderer stole it, but I never imagined anything like this would happen….' He looked in distress at Kyōzō.

'Didn't you keep the crossbow somewhere safe?'

'Well, it wasn't in a locked place. I thought it would be safe enough in my room….'

'Why do you have a crossbow in the first place?'

'My dad's hobby is hunting… But guns are dangerous, so we'd go hunting rabbits with slingshots and crossbows.'

'Slingshots? Those kids' toys?'

'Ours are quite powerful. You could take out a rabbit with just one shot if you hit it right.'

'I see. Well, what's done is done, so I suppose we shouldn't dwell too much on the matter. Anyway, where were you last night?'

'I was in my own room, asleep. I went to bed at midnight and didn't notice anything until three o'clock, and that was because of the commotion.'

Kyōzō looked Yūsaku straight in the eye. He felt confident he'd be able to detect any sign of a lie.

The man had to be lying, Kyōzō was convinced of that. Yet his years of experience as a cop told him that, in this case, Yūsaku was telling the truth.

'Did you lock your door?'

'Er, yes. I always lock the door when I'm in my room.'

'So when you're not in your room—?' asked Kyōzō... Shouldn't it be the other way around, he thought.

'I usually don't lock it then. It's such a bother taking the key with me every time I go out. You lock the door by pushing in the button in the doorknob, and closing the door. I forgot my key twice already and locked myself out, so I stopped doing it. Yet if I'd been in the habit of locking my door, my crossbow wouldn't have been stolen. But what does this have to do with the case?'

Kyōzō was lost in thought, so Okuda answered in his place.

'A great deal. At the time of the murder, you were inside your room with the door locked. You claim you were asleep, but that's a lie. You killed Mr. Kikuichirō and then attacked Mitsuko Kawamura and Yukie Hachisuka, who had witnessed the crime.'

The young man seemed bewildered for a moment, but when he finally understood what he was being accused of, he turned pale.

'Wha—what do you mean? What did I ...?'

'That's what we're about to get out of you right now. Why did you kill Mr. Kikuichirō?'

Kyōzō looked on in silence as Okuda put the pressure on Yūsaku. Something's off, he thought.

'No! It wasn't me! Why do you think I killed him!?'

Yūsaku looked at both Kyōzō and Kinoshita—who was standing near the door—pleading for help, but neither of them moved a muscle.

Okuda continued in his smug manner:

'Ms. Kawamura and Yukie claimed downstairs that they saw the murderer in this empty guest room, but that was all a lie to protect you. They saw the murderer in your room. And the person in your room, at that moment, could only have been yourself. You just told us you locked the door.'

'Yukie...? You mean, both of them said that? That the murderer was in my room?' mumbled Yūsaku in utter disbelief.

'Yep. We'll get the details from you at the police station,' said Okuda in a threatening tone. But the message had not yet sunk in.

'B—but, it's not possible. Yukie would never lie like that....'

Yūsaku kept shaking his head in disbelief.

Watching him, Okuda observed to Kyōzō:

'A kid like him will be easy once we apply some pressure. We'll take care of it at the police station, so perhaps the two of you should go back to Sakuradamon.'

Kyōzō was irritated by Okuda's obvious attempts to get rid of them, but it was also clear that the murderer had to be Yūsaku, considering the circumstances. And Division 1 was in need of help from all the men available, given the number of armed robberies of late. Just as Okuda had said, Kyōzō should leave the rest of the case to him.

'I suppose you're right. We'll leave,' said Kyōzō, getting up. Startled, Yūsaku looked straight at the inspector.

'No, don't go! I didn't do it! I really didn't do it!'

Kyōzō stared at him for a while, but then he shrugged and followed Kinoshita out of the room.

5

'Something's fishy,' muttered Kyōzō as he drank from the coffee Shinji Hayami had poured for him.

That evening, Kyōzō had stopped by Sunny Side Up, the coffee shop run his younger brother Shinji. The interior was made to suit young women's tastes, as there was a girls' high school in the neighbourhood. Accessories were hanging neatly from the ceiling here and there and a felt-tip pen and memo pad had been placed on every table.

'What's fishy?'

Shinji was busy polishing the glasses and didn't even look at his brother.

'The murder! Didn't you listen to what I just told you?'

'Ssssttt! Don't talk about your cases here! What if Ichio hears you, she'll never go back to work!' said Shinji, putting his finger to his lips, but it was already too late. Ichio, their younger sister, had sneaked out of the kitchen in the back, where she was supposed to be working, and was standing behind Shinji.

'...So you're working on a murder.'

'Aaah! .... So you heard.' Shinji almost dropped a glass.

Shinji Hayami, 26 years old. Single. Owner of a coffee shop. Height: 1.80 metres. Weight: 65 kilograms. According to the female high school students frequenting the shop, he looks exactly like a young DeNiro when he smiles. He practices basically no sports. His hobbies are cooking, watching films and reading. His parfaits are extremely well received, but according to Ichio, they only have volume going for them.

Ichio Hayami. Fourth year student at K University. Part-timer at the coffee shop. Height: 1.68 metres. Weight: ?? Practices most of the trendy sports, but is especially fond of skiing. Each season, she goes out "in search of the perfect guy," but it appears she hasn't had much luck so far. Her name Ichio might need some explanation.

Old-fashioned Japanese names for men often include numerals to indicate in which order they were born. The name Ichirō for example includes the number *ichi*, or 1, so that is a name for a first-born son, while the name Shinji contains the numeral for 2, *et cetera*. But when Kyōzō was first born, their father came out with an idiotic scheme: he planned to have three sons, but he'd give them these old-fashioned numbered names in reverse order. He had also decided on the three names: Kyōzō, which contained the numeral 3, was for his first born, Shinji for his second and Ichirō for his third son. The idea was that one could look all over Japan and still not find another third-born son named Ichirō. And his plan went well up to the second-born, but then the third child turned out to be a girl.

Their father could have given up at that point, but he was a stubborn man and was determined to stick to his original plan. While dad had no intention of choosing a different name for his third child, mom was only willing to comply if they picked a different reading of the name.

In the Japanese language, even names written with the exact same characters can be read in various ways. Ichirō was without doubt a male name, but using an alternative reading of the characters for Ichirō, the parents settled on the feminine-sounding Ichio. Which is how the girl came to be named Ichio Hayami.

'Let me guess.... The murder at The 8 Mansion?'

Kyōzō had no choice but to nod in agreement.

'But I heard you arrested the murderer?'

'He hasn't actually been arrested yet. He's come down to the police station voluntarily to help the police with their enquiries, as they say. But I'm sure the arrest warrant will be issued shortly.'

'So you don't think he did it?' asked Ichio, her eyes sparkling with expectation. Shinji smile wryly as he looked at her. Ever since Kyōzō had made it into Division 1, Ichio always tried to get all the details whenever a murder happened. Shinji's love of mystery fiction had apparently had a bad influence on her. As for Shinji, he thought himself smart enough not to look for the grandeur of a fictional murder in a real murder case.

'Well, it's not that I think he didn't do it… I just feel something's not quite right.'

Ichio slipped under the counter and sat down next to Kyōzō. Shinji sighed at the sight. No work would be done until she had wheedled all the information out of her brother.

At Ichio's urging, Kyōzō started explaining the outlines of the case. He normally shouldn't have been talking to his siblings about a case that hadn't been resolved yet, but he thought that if some sort of magic trick had been used, such as those featured in the mystery novels they both liked so much, he might be able to get some good ideas. He was also quite aware that both of them were good at keeping secrets.

'There are two witnesses in this case. Both of them were attacked right after the murder, delaying the report to the police. Both sustained light wounds. According to their statement, they saw someone shoot a crossbow from a certain room, but the student who uses the room claims he was in there at the time of the murder, asleep and with the door locked. The crossbow which is believed to be the murder weapon also belongs to him. As you can see, under the circumstances the police have no choice but to consider him the murderer.'

'Well then, what's your problem?'

'It's hard to say. Call it a police detective's hunch.'

Ichio held her breath for a while, but then burst out laughing.

'Did you hear that, Shin! A detective's hunch! A detective's… hunch…!'

'Stop laughing! I'm being serious here. It doesn't seem to me as though he was lying. And even if he did commit the murder, things still don't add up.'

'Such as what?' asked Shinji, as he turned the sign on the door from OPEN to CLOSED. It was still early, but he'd decided to give up on the day.

'If Yūsaku is indeed the culprit, why would he he kill a man from his own room, with his own crossbow, and then brazenly try to claim he'd locked the door and was asleep inside?'

'Perhaps he thought nobody had seen the murder… Oh, I see,' said Ichio, as she realised her mistake.

'Precisely. The murderer did know he'd been seen: he attacked both of the witnesses. That's another thing that doesn't make any sense. If it were Yūsaku, why did he merely knock them unconscious after being seen? It would make more sense to have killed them in order to silence them, or—if he didn't want to kill them—he could've simply fled the house in the meantime.' Kyōzō cocked his head.

'But the person who attacked the two witnesses doesn't have to be the murderer,' interjected Shinji, and Kyōzō frowned.

'So you're suggesting that the murderer didn't know there were witnesses, and that someone else who had nothing to do with the murder just decided to knock the two of them out? Do you really believe in such a coincidence?'

'Well, that would at least make Yūsaku's actions as the potential murderer less odd. Suppose the reason Yūsaku confessed to being in his own room was because he didn't know he'd been seen? Don't take me too seriously: I'm only suggesting a theoretical possibility. Personally, I find it more interesting that the body was moved slightly from its original position.'

'As I said, that was probably because they wanted to hide the body, but then gave up on that idea.'

'What's the point of hiding the body if two witnesses saw the murder? And considering that all the killer did was to drag the body across the floor, he could at least have dragged it down to the ground floor, even if the victim was heavy. He had almost two hours to do that.'

'So what other reason could there be for moving the body?' Kyōzō pouted unhappily.

Shinji thought in silence for a moment. 'Hmm, why would someone move a dead body…? The fact it was only moved one or two metres intrigues me.'

'Hey, how about this? There was something underneath the body, and the murderer needed to get hold of it,' proposed Ichio cheerfully.

'But they could have just flipped the body over. It didn't look like that to me,' replied Kyōzō after giving the idea some consideration.

'You know, there's *The Border-Line Case*[ii]… But I guess that wouldn't apply here.'

'What's that, what border-line?' asked Kyōzō in response to Shinji's suggestion.

'I don't suppose The 8 Mansion is built right on the border between S Ward and some other ward? No, that would be too silly. What if the body had moved itself there? No, I mean when it was still alive of course.'

'You mean could Kikuichirō have crawled there as he was dying? No, he died instantly, and there are clear marks to show he'd been dragged, so that won't work.'

'Hmm, then perhaps I shouldn't pay it too much attention, there might be nothing behind it.'

Shinji appeared to have lost interest. As he was getting off his stool, the cowbell hanging over the door rang.

'I'm sorry, we're already closed for today,' Shinji explained to the young woman who had just entered, but she showed no sign of leaving.

Kyōzō rose quickly from his seat.

'Miss Yukie....'

And Yukie Hachisuka flew straight into his arms.

CHAPTER TWO: KYŌZŌ FALLS IN LOVE

1

Shinji and Ichio watched in astonishment.

As for Kyōzō, he was nailed to the spot, with no idea of what was going on and whether he should put his arms around Yukie or not.

'But since when do you have a gir—? Oh! So spring has finally come into your life, dear brother mine! As your sister I couldn't be happier for you! Congratulations! I—I think I need to cry…,' mocked Ichio, as she made a pretence of rubbing her eyes.

'No, no, it's not like that! This is all a—.'

While Kyōzō was busily looking for an excuse, Yukie slid away from him and bowed slightly to apologise for her entrance.

'May I present Yukie Hachisuka, the daughter of the deceased Mr. Kikuichirō,' said Kyōzō with an embarrassed look on his face.

'Oh! So you only met her today, and you're already…,' said Ichio, glaring at her brother.

'I told you it's not like that! Anyway, Miss Yukie, what has happened? How did you know about this place?'

Yukie sat down on the counter seat Shinji had offered her. She placed the word processor which she had been clutching to her chest on the counter and started typing.

Kyōzō gave a sign to his siblings to explain that Yukie couldn't speak. Shinji and Ichio peered at the words on the screen.

'*I didn't know what else to do. Your colleague told me where to find you.*'

'If you tell me what's the matter, I'd be glad to help you in any way I can.'

'*Yūsaku didn't do it. Reopen the investigation please.*'

Kyōzō looked doubtful.

'You'll have to talk to Detective-Sergeant Okuda about that. As things stand, the case is already out of my hands.'

'*The detective has already made up his mind that Yūsaku did it. He won't listen to anything I have to say. Mr. Hayami, you are the only one I can rely on.*'

You are the only one I can rely on…. Kyōzō shivered with pleasure at the thought.

‘Tha—that might well be the case, but … It presents a problem….’ Kyōzō blushed slightly as he scratched his head and gazed up at the ceiling.

‘All right! I see your point. I can’t say no if you plead like that. I’ll go over the case once again myself. To tell you the truth, I was just thinking that there were a number of odd points about it that I didn’t feel should be left to Okuda.’

‘You have hearts for eyes, dear brother.’

‘Shut up!’ Kyōzō scolded his teasing sister and turned back to Yukie.

‘You don’t need to worry any more. If Yūsaku is indeed innocent, I promise you I’ll find the real murderer.’

Yukie gazed at Kyōzō and her eyes filled with tears. One ran down her cheek, but she wiped it away and tried to smile.

‘She’s beautiful,’ muttered Shinji, after they had called a taxi for Yukie and sent her back home.

‘She is beautiful, but she’s the type that can ruin a man,’ observed Ichio. Of course, both Kyōzō and Shinji knew that whenever Ichio talked about the type that could ruin a man, it meant she didn’t like the fact the other girl was better looking.

‘The poor girl, unable to speak. I think she could hear though. What’s wrong with her?’ asked Shinji. Kyōzō explained how she’d lost her vocal cords because of an accident.

‘By the way, was it really okay for you to promise you’d work on the case like that? If it turns out Yūsaku really is the murderer, she’ll hate you for it,’ said Ichio, and Kyōzō felt a chill run down his spine. In his mind’s eye, he’d already arrested the real murderer and was about to receive a warm embrace fromYukie….

Shinji followed up with another attack on their grim-faced brother:

‘Why does she care so much about this Yūsaku anyway?’

2

On the following day at ten o’clock, Kyōzō was once again joined by Kinoshita for another visit to the Hachisuka residence. The section chief hadn’t been very happy with Kyōzō’s decision, but he was now stubbornly continuing the investigation.

There were no signs of a police presence outside The 8 Mansion. It was as if nothing had ever happened there. Kinoshita pushed the intercom button on the metal gate and explained who they were, and, with a motorised noise, it opened.

A frail old lady with bags under her eyes welcomed them in the main hall. It was Tamiko Hachisuka, wife of Kikuo Hachisuka. She was wearing mourning clothes, but for some reason they appeared like normal clothing on her.

'Detectives, what brings you here today?'

'It's nothing urgent, but there are still a few points we'd like to clear up...,' said Kyōzō vaguely. 'Is everyone inside the house?'

'Well, no, actually. The Yanos are staying in a hotel at the present time.'

'And why is that?'

'I fear they couldn't bear staying here....'

Kyōzō found that altogether natural, given that their son might well have killed their employer's oldest son.

'I see. I'd like to look around the house. And, if you're not too tired, I'd like you to accompany us.'

Tamiko looked quite worn out, but she still agreed. 'Will we be going up to the second floor...?'

'Yes, but only for a quick look.'

The south wing of the ground floor consisted of the parlour, where everybody had gathered the day before, and the dining room.

They passed through the parlour and opened the French windows to access the inner courtyard. Although, in a bird's eye view, the mansion appeared to have two separate inner courtyards, there was in fact only one single courtyard at ground level. It was only the space above which had been divided in two by covered galleries connecting the east and west hallways on the first and second floor.

'So there's no connecting gallery here on the ground floor.'

'No. It would be in the way for garden parties.'

'Aaaaah!' Just at that moment, Kinoshita let out a startled cry and grabbed Kyōzō's arm.

'What's the matter?'

'O—over there!'

A gigantic St. Bernard had silently approached the two policemen and was now staring at them.

'Grrrrrrrr.' A low growl came from a huge body that was probably as heavy as Kyōzō's.

'What kind of monster is that!?'

The dog's ears twitched at the use of the word "monster," and it bared its teeth at Kinoshita.

Kinoshita edged towards the French windows.

'It's all right, Detective. He won't bite you. Just be careful he doesn't steal anything from you. He likes playing with new toys,' remarked Tamiko calmly.

It was difficult to take her at her word, given the creature's antagonistic attitude, but as long as they weren't carrying rabies, there wasn't a dog that could scare Kyōzō.

He glared at it. The dog appeared to be taken aback by the sudden turn of events. It was evidently not accustomed to being glared at by a human.

But it soon recovered from its surprise and glared back even more ferociously.

'Hmmm...,' murmured Kyōzō.

'Grrr...,' growled the dog.

The two—the dog and the human—glared at each other for a while, but then the dog looked away.

I won, thought Kyōzō.

But the expression on the dog's face said: 'Let's say that today ended in a tie,' and it returned triumphantly to the dog house. It appeared to be quite a proud dog.

'What's his name?' asked Kyōzō, expecting it to be something like Caesar or Alexander.

'His name is Hachi.'

It took some time for a reaction.

'Hachi? You mean, Hachi as in the Hachikō statue in front of Shibuya Station[iii]?'

'Well, yes, I think so. My husband wouldn't accept any other.'

And, considering the old man only built his mansion in the shape of an 8 instead of the shape of a bee because both are pronounced *hachi*, it wasn't all that surprising he was also fixated on Hachi in other matters.

'Let's go, Inspector!'

Urged on by Kinoshita, they decided to look around elsewhere.

The north wing was occupied by a large kitchen and the Yano couple's room.

'What kind of people are the Yanos?'

'All the cooking is done by Yoshie. She's a hard worker, but given what's happened...,' replied Tamiko with some regret in her voice.

'And her husband?'

'He's a bit of a countryman and can be blunt, but he does everything you ask of him perfectly.'

'And Yūsaku?'

Tamiko's face looked troubled.

'…I simply can't believe it. I thought of him as part of the family. To think he would have killed my son….'

'Was there bad blood between him and your son Kikuichirō?'

'I certainly wasn't aware of anything like that. He's a bright boy, loved by all. It had already been arranged for him to come to work at our company once he graduated. I can't believe he'd return all of that kindness with such a horrible deed.'

Tamiko remained silent for a while.

'We don't know for sure he's the murderer yet. What kind of person was your son?'

'He was a nice boy. Thoughtful and smart. Not someone to get on the wrong side of people. But he's always been unfortunate. He married the wrong woman, their child was born with a weak constitution and now she can't even speak….'

'You're talking about Yukie.' She did look rather feeble, Kyōzō thought as he followed up.

'Yes. Perhaps it's because she's always lived inside this house ever since she was small. She becomes sick easily.'

Kyōzō couldn't take any more of her disparaging remarks about Yukie.

'Shall we go up to the first floor?'

The south wing of the first floor was entirely taken up by the rooms of Kikuichirō and his wife Setsuko.

'They had separate rooms?' asked Kyōzō without thinking.

Tamiko replied bluntly:

'Things have cooled down between them.'

'Why? … Excuse me, that's a rather private matter of course, but if you wouldn't mind telling me….'

'You've already seen it for yourself. It's the drinking. When they first got married, she seemed like a nice person, but before we knew it, she started drinking more and more. Lately she's been drinking like a fish, whether it's day or night. With Yukie now grown up, I told Kikuichirō he should get a divorce. But my poor child said it was all his fault, thinking only of work and not giving her enough attention.'

'So Kikuichirō had no intention of divorcing her? Perhaps he still loved her?' asked Kyōzō. If Kikuichirō had brought up the question of divorce, that might have been sufficient motive for Setsuko to kill him, he thought.

'Absolutely not! I'm sure Kikuichirō didn't have any feelings for her anymore! It was simple pity, nothing more than that. Kikuichirō said there was no way Setsuko could ever make her way through life on her own. He was always so kind….'

Tamiko stopped, took a handkerchief from her pocket and touched it elegantly against her eyes, even though Kyōzō hadn't noticed any tears there.

Kyōzō put on a regretful expression, but wasn't about to take everything Tamiko told him at face value. There was no way a mother would ever speak ill about her deceased son, after all. He needed to hear what the wife had to say before making any judgments.

'Is Mrs. Setsuko in her room right now?'

'….She didn't go outside, so I think she'll be there.'

Tamiko knocked on Setsuko's door.

'Come in, the door is open!' said a slurred voice.

Given Yukie's age, Setsuko had to be at least forty, but she didn't look it at all. She was strikingly beautiful and might have passed for thirty, but for the miniscule wrinkles near the corners of her eyes. Setsuko must have looked exactly like Yukie when she was young. She was holding a whisky bottle in her left hand, which she placed in her mouth from time to time.

'Setsuko, it's still morning. Don't drink so much,' Tamiko reproached her coolly.

'Oh, mother, who cares? I lost my husband. Can't I even have a drink to forget my misery for a while? Hahaha…. Oh, you have police detectives with you. What do you think, does this suit me?' Setsuko asked Kyōzō as she swirled the bottom of her dress.

Kyōzō hesitated for a moment before answering.

'Yes, it suits you perfectly.'

'How wonderful! You're good at giving compliments, Mr. Detective. What was your name again?'

'Hayami.'

'And are you any good at comforting a widow?'

Kyōzō didn't know how to answer that, so he replied tactfully:

'You have my condolences. It was a terrible incident.'

Setsuko snuggled up to him with a seductive look in her eyes. She reeked of alcohol.

'Rats—that's not what I asked. I asked you… if you're good at comforting a woman.'

She placed her hands on Kyōzō and started to stroke his chest. She was becoming more aggressive by the second.

Kyōzō pulled away. '…I'm afraid I'm not very good at that, ma'am.'

'It's simple. You just sit right here and have a few drinks with me. Easy enough?'

'Er, I'm not allowed to drink when I'm on duty.'

'Oh, that's a shame. What about the boy over there, then?'

Setsuko aimed her wandering eyes at Kinoshita, who had been silently writing something in his organiser.

Kinoshita, taken aback by the sudden turn of events, raised his head slowly.

'Oh, I see you're quite handsome, now I've had a good look at you. How about it, sonny boy? Will you keep a poor widow company? No attachments, nothing, and I might even be able to teach you a thing or two….'

'Oh, er, no, you see, I-I have a girlfriend, and um, her name is Sanae, and she gets jealous easily….'

Kinoshita wasn't the stoical type. He looked desperately for an excuse as beads of perspiration appeared on his face.

'Oh, that's right. The Inspector here has no girlfriend. And considering your age, the Inspector would be a much better match!'

'Wha—what are you saying! When there's love, age doesn't matter…!'

In his confusion, Kyōzō had said more than he should. A mysterious smile—was she grieving or enjoying herself?—appeared on Setsuko's face as she watched the two detectives.

'…Nobody in this house wants to comfort me. They all think I'm not really sad. Isn't that right, mother?'

'Of course,' replied Tamiko, glaring at Setsuko.

Setsuko grinned and turned back to Kyōzō: 'See? But, in my own way, I did love my husband. You do understand, don't you, Mr. Hayami?'

Kyōzō didn't understand anything she was saying, but he naturally couldn't admit it. He was happy the conversation had made a turn, however.

'Of course I do. By the way, I realise this is not the best time, given what's happened, but I'd still like to ask you more about the case.'

Setsuko moved sullenly away from Kyōzō, placed the bottle on a side table, and slumped down into an armchair.

'...As you wish. Ask me anything you like.'

'Well then, where were you at the time your husband was killed, at around one o'clock in the morning?'

'I was asleep. Sound asleep.'

'Did you hear anything strange, or notice anything different or unusual?'

Setsuko shook her head wearily.

'Do you have any idea why your husband was murdered?'

She burst out laughing.

'None at all! I can't even believe he was killed. It'd be different if I'd been murdered! There are plenty of people in the house who'd love to get rid of me, but whoever would've guessed my husband would be the one to get bumped off? And by no less than that Yūsaku, the boy he'd taken such good care of. Life's strange, don't you think, Mr. Hayami?'

'Setsuko, stop talking nonsense to the detectives,' said Tamiko. Setsuko glared at her.

'Nonsense? What nonsense? I'm not loved by anyone in this house. I'm just a nuisance here. You think that of me yourself, mother.'

'You're not even worth the trouble of killing.'

On hearing such words from the mouth of the taciturn old woman, Kyōzō felt a chill run down his spine.

Even Setsuko appeared to be shocked. She turned pale and leant over the table as she started wailing. The whisky bottle fell on the carpet, but nothing came out of it. It was already empty.

'Out! Out of my room!'

'I'm terribly sorry, but I have one last question. I gather things weren't going well between you and your husband. What was the reason for that?'

Kyōzō didn't like having to put the question while the woman was down, but it had to be asked.

Setsuko, trembling, didn't answer.

Tamiko interjected: 'I already told you. As you can see, this woman is drinking all day....'

Kyōzō motioned to her to keep silent, and spoke once again to Setsuko.

'You have a life of luxury and a wonderful daughter. What caused you to become like this? There has to be something. Did your husband cheat on you, for example...?'

'He would never do that! Not once has he hurt her in any way!'

Setsuko's head jerked up at Tamiko's words. Her tear-ruined make-up made her look like a raccoon, but that only strengthened the resolute anger in her eyes.

'That's a lie! You don't know anything, not a single thing about what kind of man your son was! Mr. Detective, you've guessed right.'

'...So he was unfaithful to you?'

'Unfaithful? That's one way of putting it. It was some kind of disorder. Whenever he had a free moment, he would see some woman here or there....'

'And that's what caused you to hate your husband?' asked Kyōzō, as nonchalantly as possible.

'Yes! I imagined killing him with these hands more than once...,' Setsuko started to say, but then covered her mouth.

'...Why are you asking me these questions? The man's dead now. It's all over.'

'No, madam, it's not over yet. It's my job to investigate anyone with a motive for killing your husband.'

'But it's obvious that Yūsaku killed him! Anyway, that's all you'll get out of me. You can investigate all you want outside this room.'

She turned her back to Kyōzō and fell silent.

'We'll leave you be for today. But know this: I'm not convinced Yūsaku is the murderer just yet. We may call on you again,' said Kyōzō as he left.

'I hope you don't believe anything she told you,' Tamiko said as they left the room.

'I don't believe anybody at this point. I only believe in the things I see with my own two eyes.'

Kyōzō was impressed by how good his own words sounded. He decided he'd use that phrase from now on. That he hadn't noticed that Kinoshita had started making a header entitled *Babblings of The Inspector* was a good thing for both of them.

They moved to the north wing on the first floor, which housed the rooms of Kikuo and Tamiko, and the study.

Kikuo Hachisuka, master of the house, was sitting at the desk in his study, and was busy writing.

'Oh, the police. Do you need something from me?'

He welcomed Kyōzō with a smile.

'Yes, if you don't mind.'

'I see, I see. If you would take a seat there for a minute. Kikuichirō left quite a lot of work for me to get through,' said the old man, turning back to the mountain of documents on his desk and adjusting his reading glasses.

'I'll pour us some tea then. I hope black tea suits your taste?' asked Tamiko, to which Kinoshita cheerfully replied: 'I'd prefer some coffee please.' He appeared to be thirsty.

'And Mr. Hayami?'

Kyōzō shot a reproving look at Kinoshita, but said: 'I'd like some coffee too, then.'

It took Tamiko over ten minutes to bring the drinks—perhaps because Yoshie Yano wasn't there—but Kikuo still hadn't finished his work. Kinoshita took a sip of his coffee, laid some refill pages on the table and started writing on them in a cheerful manner. He was writing down the names of all the persons related to the case on their own separate page and putting them in alphabetical order.

'Too much free time,' mumbled Kyōzō.

After finishing his coffee very slowly, Kyōzō finally broke the silence.

'Ahem, Mr. Hachisuka—.'

Kikuo looked up in surprise.

'Oh! How long have you been here?'

'Excuse me? What do you mean? We spoke with each other just moments ago!'

Kikuo cocked his head to one side.

'Really? Oh, that's fine then. Splendid. Take your time.'

He turned back to his work once again, but Kyōzō quickly continued.

'Sir, could you spare us some time instead? Ten minutes will be more than enough.'

'Dear, they're here because of Kikuichirō.' Tamiko offered a helping hand as well.

'Kikuichirō? What's the matter with him?'

Kikuo looked surprised, but Kyōzō was even more astonished. Had he forgotten his own son had died?

'Did you forget, dear? He died yesterday. He was murdered.'

Kikuo cried out in shock: 'What did you say! Kikuichirō was murdered? If he's not here anymore, I'll have to check the documents myself instead! As if I don't have enough to do....'

Tamiko showed no signs of annoyance, but spoke to her husband as one would talk to a child.

'But dear, you're going through those documents right now.'

Kikuo looked down at the papers spread across his desk as if it were the first time he had seen them.

'Oh, you're right. And who might these gentlemen be?'

'They're the police. You met them yesterday, remember?'
Kikuo appeared to be digging in the depths of his memory, but didn't seem to remember them.
'Guess the old man's going senile,' Kinoshita whispered in Kyōzō's ear, and he wrote down "Senile Old Man" on the page for Kikuo in his organiser.
Kyōzō had started to nod when the old man burst out:
'What did you say!? I am absolutely not going senile! Who do you think I am? I am Kikuo Hachisuka, director of Hachisuka Construction! Hachisuka Construction can build anything!'
Although he was no longer expecting much, Kyōzō decided this was the moment to start with his questions:
'Do you remember what happened yesterday?'
He glanced at Kinoshita beside him, who was scribbling in his organiser again. "BE CAREFUL: EXTREMELY SHARP EARS."
Kikuo snorted at what he considered a foolish question by Kyōzō.
'Of course I remember. I had a fried egg and fish for breakfast, as always. Miso-broiled mackerel I think it was. And miso soup with tofu.'
Kinoshita was busily writing "Breakfast: fried egg and miso-broiled mackerel."
'Excuse me, you said there was tofu in your miso soup?' Kinoshita asked Kikuo, while scratching his head with the back of his pen. Kyōzō said firmly:
'Forget about that! Mr. Hachisuka, what I want to ask you is—.'
'I don't know why, but we had filled rice balls for lunch. It's not as if we were out on a picnic—.'
'I am asking you about the time Kikuichirō was murdered!' yelled Kyōzō. Surprised, Kikuo stopped talking.
'…Please, Mr. Hachisuka. What were you doing around one o'clock in the morning?' said Kyōzō carefully, posing his question slowly so that there would be no mistake.
'One in the morning? That's the middle of the night. Do you really think I'd be having a meal at that time?' He was looking at Kyōzō as if he had been accused of being a fool.
'…Well, if you were not having a meal, what were you doing then, sir?'
Kyōzō was on the verge of an explosion, but patiently continued his questioning.
Kikuo cocked his head in thought.

'...I was probably sleeping. Right, dear?' he asked Tamiko, and she nodded.

Kyōzō sighed. So he'd have to take Tamiko at her word.

'Were you also asleep at that time? Did you perhaps notice something unusual?'

'No. I was sound asleep until I was woken at three. I think my husband's the same.'

'Mr. Hachisuka, do you know whether anyone had a grudge against Kikuichirō?'

'Someone with a grudge against him? No, I know of no one.'

Kyōzō was relieved that, for once, he'd got a straight answer. But as always, the answer was not useful at all.

'Saeki knows much more about Kikuichirō, you should ask him.'

'Saeki? Oh, his secretary. Were they on good terms?'

'I think so. Kikuichirō was always praising him.'

Kyōzō decided that trying to get more out of the old man would be pointless.

'Let's go up to the second floor then. Mr. Hachisuka, thank you for your time.'

By the time Kyōzō was on his feet, Kikuo Hachisuka, who had not moved one inch from his seat, was snoring.

3

The room on the south-east corner of the second floor was occupied by Kikuji Hachisuka, the second son.

There was no reply to her knock, but Tamiko didn't wait to open the door.

Kikuji's room was coordinated in black and white, from the furniture to the blinds. It gave the room a clean, but sterile atmosphere. What sprang immediately to the eye was his brand new AV system and the shelf filled with videotapes. The moment Kinoshita entered the room, he practically drooled over the machine. However, there was no sign of Kikuji himself in the room.

'Kikuji?' Tamiko cried out, and a voice came from the bathroom.

'Mother? Wait a sec.'

Kyōzō was quite surprised at Kikuji's appearance, as he dried his head with a towel. He had been told that Kikuji was around forty, single and unemployed, so he had imagined the man would have a sleazy appearance.

Kikuji, however, turned out to be a handsome man who looked somewhat like Clark Gable. He himself was perhaps aware of the resemblance, as he, too, sported a moustache. His crimson nightclothes suited him well.

Kyōzō's first impression of Kikuji was that of a smug individual, further confirmed when he noticed the man's luxuriant black hair.

Perhaps this is my murderer, he thought to himself.

'Oh, mother, you look awful. You didn't get a wink of sleep last night, did you? With what happened to Kikuichirō....'

'You, on the other hand, look as though nothing happened,' retorted his mother. Kikuji reacted with a visibly hurt expression: 'I'm quite shocked by his death myself, too. It's just that I recovered more quickly. With the condition father is in, I'm the one who has to keep things going for us all.'

'Silly you, nobody's expecting anything from you.'

Kikuji shrugged in response to Tamiko's comment, and flashed an embarrassed smile to Kyōzō. He threw the towel on the bed, sat down on a divan and placed his feet on an ottoman.

'Let's stop fighting in front of the detectives. And what do you want from me, gentlemen?'

Kyōzō thought he'd have a bit of fun with him first.

'Mr. Kikuji, may I ask what is your occupation?'

'Oh, I don't have what you might call an occupation.... I speculate a bit....'

'Just admit it's gambling,' corrected Tamiko coldly.

'...All right. You might call it gambling. I can't get anything past my mother.'

He spread his arms out wide like a foreign film actor and smiled at Kyōzō, as if they were in it together. Kyōzō looked back at him dryly and continued his questions.

'So I assume that when you were short of money, your father or your brother would help you out?'

Kikuji seemed to take offence. He took a lighter and a packet of cigarettes from the pocket of his nightclothes and lit one.

'Are you married?' Kyōzō fired another question.

Kikuji grinned and shook his head.

'Haha, no. I wouldn't dream of it. Marriage is for barbarians.'

'For barbarians?'

Kyōzō's interests were piqued by this unexpected answer.

'Of course. Inspector, are you yourself married?'

Kyōzō frowned and shook his head.

‘Splendid! Let me explain then. You see, in the end, love is always a fleeting sensation. That is what makes love beautiful. But the institution of marriage completely ignores that fundamental truth. What is there for a couple when their love has disappeared? Disillusion. That’s all they’re left with. To put it bluntly, marriage is nothing more than sacrilege against love. Don’t you agree?’

‘But… there are plenty of couples who love each other until death,’ said Kyōzō, disapprovingly.

‘I still love your father very much,’ added Tamiko, but Kikuji waved their objections away.

‘There are probably couples who do love each other. But there are also couples who only think they are still in love with each other. But that is simply because they choose to think like that. Because they know they’ll have to live together forever. They have to love each other, or else tomorrow would be unbearable. And those who can’t fool themselves eventually divorce.’

Whilst Kikuji’s views were extreme, Kyōzō thought he did have a point. As he considered the argument, Kinoshita poked him.

‘Inspector!’ he whispered in Kyōzō’s ear, as he suddenly remembered he hadn’t come to talk about that. He coughed once.

‘I see your point about marriage. Shall we continue with my questions now? Where were you last night around one in the morning?’

‘I was asleep of course. I didn’t hear anything, I didn’t see anything. But I am sure I already told the other detective that—.’

Kyōzō continued his questions, despite the comment.

‘Do you know anybody who might hold a grudge against your brother, or who would benefit from his death?’

‘Nobody in particular, but if I had to name someone, I’d say my sister-in-law, Setsuko. But isn’t the murderer Yūsaku?’

‘At this point, everyone is still a suspect. Including yourself.’

‘Me? And why would I want to kill my brother?’ asked Kikuji, although he didn’t seem offended by the implication.

‘I can think of plenty of motives.’

‘For example?’ asked Kikuji mockingly.

‘For example… what comes to mind first, of course, is the matter of inheritance. By killing Kikuichirō, your share of your father’s inheritance would grow.’

‘Ha! That’s nonsense. I am quite satisfied with the life I have now. And, supposing I had been in need of some money in a hurry, I’d have killed my father instead. Doesn’t that make more sense? My father might be going senile, but he's in good health, so who knows how long he'll stick around? Do you really think I'd commit a murder for a sum of money I wouldn't even know when I'd get my hands on?'

Whilst Kikuji's reasoning was rather radical, he did have a point.

'What about a grudge then? You might be suffering from a brother complex, as you've been compared to him ever since you were a child...'

Kikuji burst into laughter.

'...That's a good one! Inspector, you should have become a writer! Japanese audiences lap up dark stories like that!'

This man won't budge no matter what I say, Kyōzō realised, and he gave up.

'I see. You have no motive for the murder. Let's keep it at that for the moment. Anyway, does this also hold for Yūsaku? Was there perhaps some trouble between him and Kikuichirō?'

'Trouble... To my eyes they seemed to get along quite well.'

At the moment, it appeared only Setsuko had something of a motive. The people at S Police Station were probably busy digging deep into possible motives for Yūsaku as well, and might already be on the trail of something.

Kyōzō happened to look out out of the window, and noticed that he could see Yūsaku's room precisely opposite Kikuji's, through the windows of the gallery. He went over to the window, opened it and stuck his head out to look around.

'That's Yūsaku's room over there on the other side of the gallery, isn't it? Who else lives here on this floor?'

'Yukie lives in the room furthest to the west of this wing. And in the north wing, there's Miss Kawamura, who lives in the room also furthest to the west. Saeki, my brother's secretary, lives next to her.'

Kyōzō looked at the walls of the house facing the inner courtyard for a while, and then looked down at the courtyard itself, but couldn't see anything of importance.

'Thank you for your time. That's all for today.'

The three were about to leave the room, when Kikuji called out to them from behind.

'Inspector, correct me if I'm wrong, but I suspect you're in love yourself. And in a one-sided love, no less.'

Kyōzō turned around slowly to conceal how startled he was.

'And what makes you think that?'

'Nothing really. You were interested in my views on marriage, yet you didn't ask any questions. That is why I think you yourself weren't that far yet. I warn you, even if you do get along with this girl of yours, do not under any circumstances make the mistake of marrying her.'

'I'll consider your advice.'

Once they were out of the room, Kinoshita asked in surprise: 'Inspector, are you really in love?'

'Shut up!' barked Kyōzō.

4

Kazuo Saeki's room was the complete opposite of Kikuji's. There was no television, no radio, and the only notable piece of furniture was a large bookcase. It was filled completely with business books and study books for diplomas and other certifications.

'My name is Kazuo Saeki. I was the vice-president's secretary. Nice to meet you.'

Saeki bowed deeply as he presented his business card. He was neatly dressed in a black suit, complete with necktie. His finely-featured face and fair complexion gave him an intelligent appearance. The quintessential efficient secretary.

Kyōzō felt relieved the moment he saw Saeki. It was as if ages had passed since he had last met a normal person in the house. A strange senile old man, a lewd woman whose only pastime was drinking, and a gambler.... To be honest, he'd had more than enough of meetings with peculiar people.

'Mr. Saeki... It's quite unusual to have a secretary living inside the house, isn't it?'

'Not at all. Having a secretary at hand at all times is quite convenient in the case of someone as busy as the vice-president.'

'You appear to be quite young. May I ask how old you are?'

'Twenty-nine.'

'Oh, that's a surprise. By the way, who will become the vice-president now?'

'Well, that's something I don't know. Mr. Kikuichirō was very competent at his work and as he had no health problems, the issue was never raised.'

'But the number of potential candidates must be quite limited.'

'Well, yes, but I don't see how that's related to this case?'

'I am just suggesting that someone might possibly have committed a murder to become the vice-president of Hachisuka Construction.'

Saeki was taken aback by the answer.

'But... I thought Yūsaku was the murderer?'

'Yes, at the moment, that's certainly how things appear. However, even if he were the murderer, there's still the possibility someone else was behind it all, pulling the strings.'

Kyōzō was voicing an idea that had just crossed his mind, but now it occurred to him that it might indeed be the truth. Yūsaku appeared at present to have no motive, but just suppose someone else had asked him, or even forced him to commit the murder…? But wait, that still wouldn't explain his strange behaviour….

'By the way, where were you yesterday, at one in the morning?'

'I was asleep of course.'

'Did anything out of the usual happen?'

'Nothing in particular….'

'How was Mr. Kikuichirō as a boss?'

'…He was a very energetic man. It was quite difficult keeping up with all the work. But of course, that's what also made it so rewarding. I feel very blessed to have been hired by him,' answered Saeki, choosing his words carefully.

'…And how were things between you privately?'

'We didn't talk about anything besides work.'

'Not at all? But you lived and worked here in the same house. You must have talked about something else besides work.'

'No, he hardly talked with me about anything else. I don't think he considered me a particularly interesting person to talk to.'

Kyōzō took another good look at Saeki.

'So your impression was that he didn't think you were an interesting person?'

'Correct,' replied Saeki unflinchingly.

'And what makes you think that was the case?'

'Because he once told me that in so many words. That I was boring.'

'And why did he say that?' asked Kyōzō, driven by curiosity.

'The vice-president had had quite a lot to drink at the time…. We were at a karaoke club, and he ordered me to sing something too, so I had no choice. It was then that he told me I was boring.'

'What did you sing?'

'I think it was *The Moon Over the Castle Ruins*[iv],' answered Saeki placidly.

This guy is pretty strange, too.

Kyōzō felt a chill run down his spine.

Saeki's room was separated from Yūsaku's room by the empty guest room they had been shown the day before. Saeki lived closest to Yūsaku, but it would have been impossible for him to climb out of his window over to Yūsaku's room, high above the inner courtyard.

It was to be their last stop, so, after a tired-looking Tamiko had opened the door to Yūsaku's room for them, Kyōzō told her she need not stay any longer. She left them and went downstairs with a heavy tread.

The soft afternoon sun was shining into Yūsaku's residence as the two detectives entered.

It was well-lit, but to ensure he wouldn't miss anything, Kyōzō switched the light on anyway. Touching the light switch left some white powder, used to identify fingerprints, on his own finger. The police had already checked whether there were any prints other than Yūsaku's there.

Kyōzō's first impression was that it was the room of a university student with no money problems. The furniture—a bed, desk and bookcase among others—appeared to have been bought together as one set. There was also a 14-inch television, and a radio cassette player with a built-in CD player. The bed and other furniture pieces had been placed against the walls, leaving the space in front of the window free.

'If someone could somehow have made their way in here, could they have committed the crime without Yūsaku noticing?' muttered Kinoshita, showing he was not completely brainless.

'Hmmm… Even if someone could have got in without making any noise, they would still have had to open the window. And they couldn't have done much about the noise of a crossbow being fired. But then again, there are people who won't wake up, even if you scream right next to their ear.'

It seemed less and less likely that any person besides Yūsaku could have entered this room and killed Kikuichirō. Kyōzō frowned as he realised that things were looking quite bad for Yūsaku, but he kept focused on his investigation.

The door—like all the other doors in this house—was made of sturdy plywood and fitted tightly without leaving any gaps between it and the frame. No thread, let alone a thin plastic card, could have been inserted between them, making the old "needle and thread" trick quite impossible. As Yūsaku had told them, the door could be locked by clicking in the push button on the doorknob. Kyōzō remembered that

Yūsaku had also told him he always locked the door when he was in his room.

'Kinoshita, you do the walls. I'll take the bathroom.'

The bathroom was like those to be found in any business hotel, with a built-in bath-and-shower module. Kyōzō loved to relax in a bath tub so, given the choice, he would rather go to a public bath house than sit cramped in such a small bath module.

Those darned Western individualist values, he muttered to himself.

There was, however, no opening in the bath module that a human being could pass through, as it had been cast in one piece. There was however, an opening in the ceiling, fifty centimetres square. When Kyōzō lifted the flap, he saw that, while it connected to the loft, only a small child could have passed through. It would have been impossible for any member of the household to do so.

Kyōzō exited the bathroom and went over to the window, which Kinoshita had opened and was looking down at the inner courtyard.

'The walls?'

'I didn't find anything. It's all concrete. Very sturdy, too. I was just wondering whether someone could have climbed in from the window of the empty room next door....'

'I see. Try it out.'

The younger detective turned to look at Kyōzō with an expression of utter disbelief.

'Bu—but this is the second floor. One mistake, and I'm toast—.'

Kyōzō laughed loudly.

'You'll be okay as long as you don't fall on your head. Don't worry, I'll grab you if you fall.'

'...I'll have to decline, Inspector. You're in much better shape and....'

'Do you really think you'd be able support my weight? Stop making excuses and go. Besides, you haven't done one single thing the whole day. Make yourself useful for a change.'

Kyōzō grabbed Kinoshita by the collar like a cat, and tried to push him through the window.

'I—Inspector, don't let go of me. I still want to live for another sixty years at least. If I die, I'll be haunting you till the day you die, I swear. I'm not kidding.'

Kinoshita was still trembling after taking his slippers off, but he began to lean slowly out of the window, his right hand tightly gripping Kyōzō's [v].

He reached out for the other window with his left hand, but it was too far away. Left without a choice, he removed his left leg from Yūsaku's window sill and edged it towards the other window. He was only supported by his right hand and leg now.

'Don't look down.'

Kyōzō's unnecessary comment inevitably made Kinoshita look.

It was only five or six metres to the ground, but it was enough to make him feel faint.

'I—Inspector! It's impossible! Yūsaku did it! That's the only way!' whined Kinoshita as he tried to crawl back.

'Don't be such a coward! How did a cry-baby like you ever become a cop!?' Kyōzō yelled back.

'I don't care! I'll go back to the countryside and take over my parents' grocery shop!'

'Enough talk! Get a move on or I'll push you out!'

Alarmed by Kyōzō's threat, Kinoshita once again stretched out his arm and leg.

Afraid of being pushed out, he extended his left leg to show how hard he was trying. The end of his sock barely managed to reach the window next door. With that small support for his foot secured, he attempted to reach the window with his left hand as well.

'I did it, Inspector, I did it!'

Kyōzō let go of Kinoshita, who was now hanging between the two windows with his limbs stretched out like a spider.

'Wha—what should I do now?'

'Open the other window and climb inside.'

Thinking he had already conquered his greatest obstacle, Kinoshita didn't protest this latest order, and tried to apply force through his left hand to open the window.

At that very moment, Kyōzō remembered something, but it was already too late. Kinoshita's foot slipped and he fell, screaming at Kyōzō.

'Noooooo, curse you!'

A loud thud followed.

When Kyōzō finally dared to look down, he saw that Kinoshita was lying sprawled out on top of an azalea shrub. He appeared to be still alive. The windows of the various rooms of the house were open, and surprised faces were looking down on the inner courtyard to see what had happened.

A gigantic figure pounced on the wriggling Kinoshita.

It was the dog Hachi. Hachi licked Kinoshita's face for a while and tugged at his clothes, but when he found Kinoshita's organiser lying next to him, the dog triumphantly took it with him in his mouth.

Kyōzō cupped both hands around his mouth and shouted: 'Kinoshita, I'm sorry! I forgot that window was locked!'

CHAPTER THREE: SHINJI SPEAKS HIS MIND

1

'He hasn't broken anything, it seems. Just a sprain. But he's covered with bruises and scratches, of course,' said the doctor.

Kinoshita had been whining about how his leg was broken and how his whole body was bruised, so Kyōzō had taken him to a nearby hospital.

'But he needs to give that leg some rest for a couple of days,' concluded the doctor. Kyōzō clicked his tongue. Kinoshita was sure to use the doctor's advice as an excuse to take some time off. It was a busy period for Division 1, so it wasn't likely the chief would appoint a replacement detective to the case. And, if things got worse, Kyōzō himself could be taken off the case as well.

Kinoshita acted the part of the patient in pain, so Kyōzō reported the accident to headquarters and drove him back home.

Kinoshita sulked all the way in the car and refused to look at Kyōzō.

Kyōzō couldn't take it anymore, and said: 'You know, Kinoshita, it's as much your fault as mine. You were there with me all the time. You heard Okuda tell us that the door and the window in that room were locked, didn't you?'

'I suppose that's true, but....'

'Anyway, I'm glad you're okay. And we know for sure now that the only way into Yūsaku's room is through the door.'

'Are you going to see the Yanos now, Inspector?'

'Yes, that's the plan. Are you coming along? You want to know how this case ends, don't you?'

Kinoshita's leg conveniently started to hurt again.

'Oh, my leg hurts sooooo much. I'd love to come with you, sir, of course, but I'd only be a burden like this....'

'Oh, all right. And here I was thinking we'd have a nice lunch first,' replied Kyōzō nonchalantly. Kinoshita carefully weighed his options. It was clear that a brutal fight was going on in his mind.

'Now you mention it, it's been a long time since I last had so' sushi...,' Kinoshita muttered to himself. Kyōzō grinned. The negotiations had started.

'Ramen noodles.'

'Yakiniku grilled meat,' countered Kinoshita immediately. Perhaps he had started his bid high on purpose.

'Ramen noodles.' Kyōzō wasn't willing to concede.

'Freshwater eel.'

'Ramen noodles.'

'Tonkatsu deep-fried cutlet?'

'Ramen noodles.'

Kinoshita gave up.

'All right, ramen it is. But only the juicy pork slice noodles they serve at Keika. I won't accept any others.'

'It's settled then.'

Elated by the successful business deal, Kyōzō suddenly made a U-turn, only realising afterwards that it hadn't been necessary, since they had already been heading towards Shinjuku.

2

After their ramen noodle lunch, the two detectives headed for the hotel in S Ward to see the Yanos. They called at the front desk and went up to their room.

Yoshie Yano immediately opened the door for them, as if she had been waiting for the knock. She was a plump, friendly looking woman—the sort of person you could meet countless times, but still not remember.

'Oh, Mr. Detective. Thank you so much. I heard you were reinvestigating the case of our poor Yūsaku. Miss Yukie told us, and we've been waiting for you....'

Kyōzō had to wait for a pause in the torrent of gratitude.

'You're Yūsaku's mother, correct?'

'Yes. My name is Yoshie. Well, say something!'

The remark was addressed to a man with a dull, bearded face standing behind her, Takao Yano.

'Greetings, Inspectors. Did Yūsaku really do it?'

'What are you saying! Don't you believe your own son?!'

'I do want to believe him, but....'

Kyōzō interrupted the squabbling.

'We're investigating right now whether he did it or not.'

The four of them sat down.

Kinoshita patted his pockets and cried: 'Eh? It's gone!'

He was probably looking for his organiser. Kyōzō was about to tell him the dog had eaten it, but then thought better of it. He thought it would be better if Kinoshita stopped carrying the thing around.

'Sir, have you seen my organiser?'

'Nope,' replied Kyōzō immediately, and proceeded to question the couple.

'First I wanted to ask you about the keys you carry with you.'

No sooner had Kyōzō spoken the words than a pained expression appeared on Takao's face: 'It's only because I took the keys with me that poor Yūsaku's....'

'Where do you usually keep your keys?'

'When I was in our room, I hung them on the wall. When I was out, I usually took them with me,' was the reply.

'Was it possible for someone to have made a copy of the keys recently? For example, could someone have visited you in your room, taken one of the keys in secret, and later returned it?'

'Nobody came into our room except Yūsaku.'

'Well then... In which pocket do you keep the keys?'

'I don't keep them in my pocket. I hang the key ring on my belt.'

'So I assume that would make it impossible for someone to take them as they were walking past?' asked Kyōzō doubtfully. As he expected, Takao shook his head firmly.

'Definitely not possible.'

'I see. Did anyone ever borrow your keys for a while?'

'Not since the house was finished.'

Kyōzō remembered something.

'I understand that the room next to Yūsaku's room is kept empty? Has anybody stayed there? Wouldn't you have handed that key to them?'

'Well, we have had some guests there, but I've never handed them any keys. Most of them didn't have any bags with them, and only stayed one night.'

They had reached a dead end. Only this man, Yoshie or Yūsaku could have entered Yūsaku's room or the room next door.

'Did your wife ever have any spare keys made?' asked Kyōzō, just to be sure, but Yoshie resented the implication.

'Are you suspecting me of the murder? Why would I kill Mr. Kikuichirō?'

'I wasn't accusing you of anything. I was just considering the possibility the murderer could have obtained the keys through you indirectly.'

'I swear I never had any spare keys made.'

As the discussion went on, Kyōzō realised that he must also consider the possibility that someone could have copied Yūsaku's own key.

He made a mental note to ask Yūsaku himself.

'Let's leave the issue of the keys for now. Mrs. Yano, could I ask you where you were around the time of the murder?'

'My husband still hadn't returned by midnight, so I went to bed first.'

'So when your husband returned—.'

'I woke up. It was around a quarter past two in the morning. I remembered because I looked at the clock and scolded him.'

'Is that correct?' asked Kyōzō, and Takao nodded.

'And you were both asleep until Misses Kawamura and Yukie woke you up again to report the murder.'

'Yes.' Both Yanos nodded.

'Did you notice anything unusual on the night of the murder?'

This time they both shook their heads.

'Mr. Yano, at what time did you leave the house?'

'It was after everybody had gone to their rooms, so I think it was soon after eleven.'

'You went out for a drink. Where did you go?'

Takao told Kyōzō the name of the bar.

'What time did you arrive there?'

'It takes at least fifteen minutes, so I'd say around half past eleven.'

'And you remained there until around two?'

'...Probably,' Takao said, without much confidence. He had probably been drunk. Takao's memory might not be clear, but he could always ask the people at the bar, thought Kyōzō.

'By the way, do you know if there was any strife between Yūsaku and Mr. Kikuichirō?'

'No, absolutely not! Our son had great respect for Mr. Kikuichirō. He was even given a job! There was no trouble between them at all,' Yoshie nearly shrieked.

It did indeed seem as though she knew nothing, but Kyōzō also knew she wasn't likely to say anything disadvantageous about her son anyway. He decided he had asked enough questions.

'I see. I think that's all for today. By the way, how long do you expect to stay here?'

‘Until Yūsaku is proved innocent. But if he is actually charged with the murder, I very much doubt we’ll ever return to that house,’ said Yoshie with an agonised expression.

Kyōzō got up, and Kinoshita managed to stand up as well. It appeared as though his pain was not all performance.

After they left the hotel the two detectives went to the bar Takao Yano had visited and checked his alibi. He had indeed arrived around half past eleven and had stayed there drinking until they’d thrown him out at two in the morning to close the bar.

3

The two detectives entered the S Police Station and, after asking around, they finally found Okuda outside one of the interrogation rooms, puffing a cigarette. He wore a tired expression.

‘Is Yūsaku still inside?’ asked Kyōzō, and Okuda nodded unpleasantly.

‘Yes. The kid is really stubborn....’

‘And your arrest warrant?’

Okuda didn’t answer the question, but asked another instead: ‘And what brings you here today?’

‘Nothing. I was just nearby. Have you found out anything about his motive?’ asked Kyōzō. Okuda replied boastfully: ‘We’ve had our successes. It turns out that the previous head of the Yano family—Takao’s father—used to own a big piece of land somewhere in Hachiōji here in Tōkyō, and seems to have been quite a big shot. But after Hachisuka Construction bought all the land up, it all went downhill from there and you can see for yourself what’s become of the family since.’

‘So you mean that Hachisuka Construction used underhanded methods to acquire the land?’

‘No, nothing like that. There was nothing wrong with the deal, legally or ethically, but I wouldn’t be surprised if Takao or Yūsaku might have thought otherwise, and might have decided to vent their frustration on the wrong guy.’

‘But why would either of them act now, after all this time? And even if Takao were holding a grudge against the Hachisuka family, it’s a whole different story with Yūsaku: he’s been brought up with the Hachisukas ever since he was a kid. And they didn’t treat him coldly either, so I think that your story is rather weak as regards motive....’

'...Who cares? As long as we can say something about motive, everything will be fine. You do understand why, don't you? 'Cause nobody else could've done it.' Irritated by Kyōzō's question, Okuda had blurted out his true views of the case.

'Anyway, I need to talk to Yūsaku. Let me in.'

Okuda hesitated for a while, but gave up with a feeble protest and let the two detectives inside. Yūsaku Yano looked fatigued, as if he were about to slide off the chair he was sitting in.

Even though there may have been a few breaks, it was clear he must have been sitting there for a very long time. Okuda must have known he couldn't keep Yūsaku there forever just as a witness, so he was probably getting impatient too.

'Yūsaku, do you remember me? The name's Hayami.' As Kyōzō spoke to Yūsaku, a spark of life returned to his eyes. Kyōzō decided to finish his business as quickly as possible.

'Are you a heavy sleeper?'

'...What... do you mean?' Yūsaku blinked his eyes at the unexpected question.

'What I mean is, if someone had entered your room through the door or window, would you have woken up?'

Yūsaku glared for a second at Okuda, then answered: 'I see. But in any case, I did not wake up.'

'But what I want to know is whether you are an especially light, or perhaps a very heavy sleeper.'

'...I guess I'm just normal. I'm pretty sensitive to earthquakes though.'

'All right. And now about your key. The key to your room. Have you ever given your key to anybody, or perhaps a copy?'

Yūsaku appeared to search his memory, then shook his head wearily.

'Think carefully. If you didn't do it, then....'

'Inspector! What are you sugges—?' Okuda started to protest, but Kyōzō ignored him.

'If you didn't do it, then that means somebody else has to be in possession of your key. Nobody could have used the keys your father carries with him, so your own key is the only other explanation. Well? Perhaps you forgot it somewhere once?'

Yūsaku sighed and shook his head once more.

'I'm sorry, but nothing like that ever happened. Nobody else has even touched my key.'

It was at that very moment that Kyōzō became convinced Yūsaku hadn't done it.

'What is the meaning of this!? He was this close to confessing!'

Kyōzō answered Okuda's continuing protest with a cold look.

'Let me warn you: you'd better forget about arresting him. Not unless you want to make a murderer out of an innocent person.'

'What? But I told you that nobody else could've entered Yūsaku's room—.'

'Precisely. The circumstances are extremely grim-looking for Yūsaku. But do you really believe this boy is lying to us? He swears to us nobody else could've used his key despite his own desperate situation. I trust him. If he's tried right now, he might be convicted, I admit. But even so, I believe him.'

'Bah! So that's how you climbed the ladder, by stealing the hard work done by others. It's all clear to me now,' said Okuda resentfully. He was afraid Kyōzō would arrest Yūsaku himself later. Kyōzō looked at him with pity.

'I shudder at the thought that someone like you can be a police officer, someone so unwilling to believe in other people. And let me give you one last piece of advice. Brush your teeth. Every day. Your breath smells awful.'

Kyōzō left a speechless Okuda behind in the interrogation room.

'I'm completely stuck.'

A desperate Kyōzō was visiting Sunny Side Up after closing time.

'What are you crying about, after just one day of investigation! If you give up now, you'll remain single for the rest of your life!' said Ichio as she fiercely patted her big brother's back.

'Oh, you're right of co— Wha—what did you say? Stupid! It's not because of her that I—'

'Okay, okay, don't mind me. So, what did you learn today?'

Kyōzō briefly explained all that had happened.

'….So suppose we accept that Yūsaku didn't do it, then his father might have fabricated his alibi in some manner, or….'

'Or?'

Ichio glanced at Kyōzō's face for a second. 'Or the two witnesses lied. But I don't suppose you want to hear that.'

'Yukie lying?…. Absolutely not! Why would she lie to us!?'

'But those two have already lied once, isn't that so?'

'Yes, but… they wanted to protect Yūsaku!'

'Perhaps they lied knowing perfectly well their lie would be exposed anyway. Suppose the two of them are conspiring to frame Yūsaku for the murder, but in order to make it all sound more convincing, they first tell a lie. And when that's exposed they act all innocent, claiming they'd only lied to protect Yūsaku. Nobody would suspect that their new story was also a fabrication too, would they?'

Kyōzō opened his mouth to counter the argument, but nothing came out.

'Shi—Shinji! Tell your sister she's wrong!'

Shinji had been grinning as he watched the two from his small seat behind the counter.

'Ichio isn't being serious either, I suspect. Don't you see she's just teasing you?' he said. 'But if I were to seriously object to that theory, I'd simply say it's unlikely Yukie would kill her own father, or help anyone who did. The fact is that, if she were planning to frame Yūsaku, she'd hardly come to you to ask you to reinvestigate the case, would she? That should be enough to convince you.'

Ichio raised her hands in defeat.

'Okay, okay, I get it, pretty girls don't kill. They don't lie, they don't fart. That's how the world works, isn't it?' she said sullenly. 'Then that would mean the only possibility left is to break the alibi of that Mr. Yano—Yūsaku's father.'

'But the bar Takao Yano visited is about fifteen minutes away from the house, and the people there say he was drinking all the time, except for bathroom breaks. He was only in the bathroom for one or two minutes at a time, and there's no window for him to escape through. So he couldn't have done it.'

'I wonder,' said Shinji suggestively.

Kyōzō, surprised by his tone, asked: 'Wha—what do you mean? Do you have an idea?'

'Well, perhaps. What time was Takao Yano supposed to have been in the bar?'

'Er, from half past eleven until two. Why do you ask? The murder happened at one.'

'But did it really happen at one o'clock?'

Kyōzō had not expected the question and he weighed the suggestion in his mind. Ichio understood what Shinji was getting at right away, however.

'Aha! You're so smart, Shinji!' she said admiringly.

'Wait a second. What do you mean?'

'What I mean is, the two witnesses are the only people who say the crime happened at one o'clock, aren't they? Suppose Takao Yano had moved the clock in Yukie's room forward or backward in advance? Then, after the two of them had been knocked out, he could have gone back in the room to set the clock back to the correct time and give himself an alibi. You see it all the time—in mystery novels at least. Playing with the time of murder has been a staple in locked room murders ever since *The Big Bow Mystery*[vi]. It would also explain why those two were only knocked out and not killed. He needed them alive to vouch for his alibi.' Shinji explained his theory as if it were all basic common sense.

'So that's how it was done. And that guy was just pretending he had nothing to do with it! But it was he who did it!'

Kyōzō jumped up, causing his chair to flip over. It made a loud noise as it hit the floor.

'I'll arrest him right away!'

'Wait! You first have to check with Yukie whether someone could have tampered with her clock before the crime.'

Kyōzō had already opened the door, but he froze on the spot on hearing the name Yukie.

'…I suppose you're right. I didn't see her today, so it's a good excuse. She might have remembered something.' Kyōzō started muttering to himself.

'Perhaps you should take a bouquet?'

Kyōzō glared at the grinning Ichio, but in his mind he thought it wasn't a bad idea.

4

After locating a flower shop which was still open for business at that hour, Kyōzō bought a bouquet of roses. When he arrived at the Hachisuka residence, the wake had just finished.

This was clumsy of me, he thought, as he watched the fleet of cars driving out through the gate. It would have been unthinkable in a normal case, but as he had been away from the investigation for a short while, he had forgotten the wake would be held today.

What would people think of him, bringing a bouquet of roses to a wake? But he couldn't bear the thought of throwing away such expensive flowers.

He hid the bouquet behind his back and entered the building.

Tamiko was standing at the entrance porch, saying goodbye to the people leaving.

'Oh, Inspector. How's the young detective who was here today?'

'Kinoshita? He's fine. Just sprained his ankle. Sorry for all the commotion he caused.' Kyōzō bowed his head deeply, and the bouquet of flowers he was holding behind his back ended up in Tamiko's face.

'Oh, these roses are beautiful.'

'Eh? Roses? Ah! Oh, no, you see—.'

'How ever did you find out that Kikuichirō was fond of roses? I guess the police know everything. Thank you very much. I am sure he would've appreciated them.'

Kyōzō had no other choice but to hand them over to Tamiko.

'Yes, er, I understand very well how grieved you must be.'

Kyōzō was no good at condolences. He had memorised a few set phrases, but he always felt pathetic and never knew what to say when faced with the family of the deceased.

'I'm terribly sorry to have come on such an occasion, but I have a few questions that need to be asked. Could I perhaps see Yukie?'

'Yukie? She has just gone back to her room, so she should be there. Shall I call for her?'

'No, I think seeing her in her room would be better, actually. I know the way, so I can go alone.'

As he set off, he thought of how many bowls of ramen noodles he could have eaten with the 5000 yen he'd paid for the bouquet.

Yukie was surprised to see Kyōzō at the door, but she invited him inside and took out her word processor ready for questions.

Dressed in a suit, Yukie looked like a university student. She had a white scarf lightly wrapped around her neck.

'I met with Yūsaku today.'

Yukie had not typed anything on her word processor, but Kyōzō knew she wanted to know how Yūsaku was doing.

Feeling slightly jealous, he continued: 'They'd been interrogating him for a long time. He looked very tired. He didn't confess to the murder, but he might get arrested if he goes on like that.'

'*Can't you do anything?*'

Yukie typed anxiously on her keyboard.

'I wanted to ask you once more: do you still believe Yūsaku is innocent?'

'*Yes.*'

'Why are you so convinced of that?'

Yukie considered the question for a second and started typing again.

'*We were raised together, almost as brother and sister, ever since we were kids. I know him best. He isn't someone to tell a lie.*'

Kyōzō felt slightly relieved at reading the words "brother" and "sister."

'So you aren't lovers? For example, if you were going to be married, one could make a defence that he wouldn't go around killing your father or anything like that....'

He had dressed the one thing he wanted to know in the form of a routine question.

'*We are not lovers. I think of him as my older brother, and I'm sure he sees me as his little sister. I am sorry I couldn't be of more help.*'

Kyōzō tried to conjure a sad expression on his face while hiding his immense joy.

'You don't have to apologise for anything. Actually, I've formed a theory and came here to ask you whether it seemed plausible.'

Yukie's interest was piqued.

'You and Ms. Kawamura say the crime happened at one o'clock, but the only person who could have been in Yūsaku's room at that time is Yūsaku himself. I just confirmed that today. However, if the crime happened after two o'clock, then Yūsaku's father—Takao Yano—could have entered that room using his own keys, while Yūsaku was asleep.'

'*But it definitely happened at one o'clock.*'

'I am not saying that you both misread the clock. What I think is that someone might have set your clock back by one hour, or perhaps more.'

Yukie looked in surprise at the clock hanging on the wall, and then at her own wristwatch.

'*But my clock is giving the correct time.*'

'It is now. But the clock could have been set back to the correct time while you and Ms. Kawamura were unconscious. If my theory is correct, the two of you weren't unconscious for two hours, only thirty minutes.'

Yukie considered the possibility thoughtfully for a while, but eventually shook her head.

'*It might have been possible for somebody to tamper with the clock while I was out of the room. But both Ms. Kawamura and I wear wristwatches. One of us would surely have noticed if the clock had been showing the wrong time. I also watched the late news, and the clock was correct then. And I didn't leave my room after that.*'

Kyōzō's morale slumped as he saw the only possibility fade away.

'But then nobody could've done it! Except for Yūsaku...' he mumbled, as he started pacing up and down the room.

'To tell you the truth, I don't believe he's the murderer, either. As you say, he doesn't look like someone who would lie. But in the circumstances—!'

Kyōzō had been looking around the room absentmindedly, when his eyes fell on the drawn curtains.

'Your curtains are closed. But they were open when the murder occurred, weren't they?'

'*They were closed at first, of course. But Mitsuko peeked through them when she heard someone walking down the gallery.*'

'I see.'

Content with that explanation, Kyōzō started reconstructing the actions Mitsuko Kawamura had probably taken.

He opened the curtains slightly and peeked out, but he couldn't see Mitsuko Kawamura's room, which was exactly opposite Yukie's. The drawn curtains of one of the windows in the covered gallery blocked the view. He could, however, see the window of Saeki's room next door. The empty guest room which they might have mistaken for Yūsaku's room, however, was in a dead angle, blocked by the walls of the connecting gallery. He could vaguely make out the window of Yūsaku's room through the gallery windows. But, as the guest room next door was in a dead angle, it would have been impossible for the two witnesses to mix up the rooms.

'Was the moon out at the time?' If so, the inner courtyard would have been illuminated to a certain extent.

'*Yes.*'

'Ms. Kawamura opened the curtains like this and told you your father was outside, is that right? What did you do next?'

Yukie stood up and went over to Kyōzō, indicating they should change places.

'Was the window in the gallery—the window the crossbow arrow passed through—already open?'

'*I didn't see my father open it, so I think it was already open.*'

'Your father turned towards that window, and it was then that you saw a figure in Yūsaku's room. Was the window there open at that moment?'

She thought for a while, then nodded her head.

'*I think the window was already open.*'

'Whereabouts was that figure standing?'

Yukie took a step back. If she stuck her arm out, her wrist would reach just outside the window.

'So the figure stood that close to the window in Yūsaku's room?'

Yukie nodded vehemently.

Kyōzō considered this new fact. Why would the figure stand slightly away from the window? Although a crossbow is a powerful weapon, it would still be impossible for it to kill a person. unless you hit a vital point. Wouldn't it be more natural to lean out of the window to get as close to the target as possible?

Or perhaps the killer wanted to avoid being seen in the moonlight?

But Kyōzō immediately realised that didn't make any sense.

Why would he (assuming it was a he) be afraid of being seen by anyone? He must have seen the light in Yukie's room was on, so why risk committing the murder knowing he might be seen?

And there was another thing. The murderer had attacked Yukie and Mitsuko Kawamura, who had witnessed the crime. But why? If he wasn't going to kill them as well, why attack them in the first place? ...The trick with the clock. Shinji's theory sounded convincing. But it had been disproven now.

'Do you know how to hold a crossbow?'

Kyōzō had posed the question without giving it much thought, but Yukie jumped up and shook her head vehemently.

Kyōzō thought that was odd.

She was acting strangely. Was she hiding something? No, not Yukie!

'I think you said the figure stuck something in front of him? How did he do that?'

Kyōzō tried to get the seeds of suspicion out of his mind as he asked the question, but she tried to avoid his eyes.

No doubt about it. She was hiding something.

Kyōzō hesitated for a moment, but then decided he needed to be firm.

'...Miss Yukie. I can see you're not used to lying. Please trust me. I don't know what's troubling you, but telling me the truth is the fastest way to solve the case.'

Yukie stared at him with an agonised look. But then she let out a deep breath and reached out for her word processor.

'*I am sorry. I just couldn't tell you.*'

Kyōzō mentally willed her to continue.

'*I don't know what to do. I won't believe Yūsaku did it, but....*'

Here her hands stopped.

'But what? What are you hiding?'

Yukie hung her head down for a moment, but then started to type slowly:

'The murderer is left-handed.'

'Left-handed? You mean, they held the crossbow to their left like this?' asked Kyōzō as he acted out the part.

Yukie nodded.

'I see. And… is Yūsaku left-handed?'

'He isn't the only one. Mitsuko is also left-handed.'

'Ms. Kawamura too. But she couldn't have been the figure you two saw. Who else?'

'Only my mother.'

'Your mother? Mrs. Setsuko?'

Kyōzō could very well understand why Yukie had kept this a secret.

The testimony that the murderer was left-handed would not only incriminate Yūsaku. If Yūsaku were innocent, then suspicion would fall on her own mother.

Even if things hadn't been going well between her parents, Yukie would never want to believe her own mother had killed her father.

'Bu—but you might be mistaken. It was dark after all,' said Kyōzō, in an effort to comfort her.

'How happy I'd be if I hadn't seen it correctly. But I can still recall it clearly in my mind. The murderer held the crossbow to my right side, so to their own left.'

'Did you clearly see the crossbow?'

'Not at the time, but I have seen Yūsaku practicing with his crossbow, and looking back, the weapon did look like a crossbow.'

This was the testimony of Yukie, the girl who most of all didn't want Yūsaku to be the killer. So she was probably telling the truth, Kyōzō decided.

Setsuko had a motive for killing Kikuichirō. She appeared to be the most likely suspect after Yūsaku.

Kyōzō was standing as motionless as a stone statue, deep in thought, when there was a knock on the door and Tamiko came in carrying a tray.

'Mr. Hayami, you like coffee, I remember.'

'Oh, you shouldn't have bothered….'

'Not at all, people from the company help with everything here, so I actually have nothing else to do….'

Tamiko and Kyōzō drew up two chairs, Yukie sat on the bed and the three of them began to sip.

'When will Kikuichirō be returned to us?'

'Eh? Oh, his remains. Given that the cause of death is clear, I think the autopsy will just be a matter of form. It should be within a couple of days…,' replied Kyōzō, but Tamiko had no reaction. Had she actually been listening to him?

'Mr. Hayami.'

'Yes?'

'You don't think Yūsaku's the murderer, do you?'

'…I can't say either way, but there are some things that don't add up,' admitted Kyōzō.

'But then who is?' asked Tamiko, looking him straight in the eye.

'I have no clear suspicions at this moment, I'm sorry to say. What do you think?'

The possibility that Setsuko was the murderer had become more likely since Yukie's testimony moments ago, but Kyōzō naturally didn't mention that to Tamiko.

'Well, I don't believe Yūsaku would kill Kikuichirō, but even if he'd wanted to he's not stupid and he wouldn't have committed the murder in such a foolish way. Setsuko, on the other hand, could have lost her temper and killed Kikuichirō on impulse….'

Yukie was shaking all over. Yet Tamiko apparently had no qualms about suggesting in front of her own granddaughter that her mother may have killed her father.

'But then again, Yūsaku's crossbow was stolen a week ago, so that's hardly something done on the spur of the moment.'

Kyōzō was impressed that Tamiko showed such intelligence. He continued his questioning: 'Who you think fits the profile for this crime, then?'

'….Ms. Kawamura. She might have done it. She's a very clever woman.'

Yukie was visibly shocked by the suggestion and started moving her hands frantically.

'Yes, of course I know you're very fond of her. And I'm not saying that she did do it. You of all people know that she couldn't physically have done it.'

'And Kikuichirō's younger brother Kikuji?'

'That child can never make up his mind, so he could never act out something like this….'

There was almost a tone of disappointment in her statement.

'And the Yano couple?'

'Perhaps if they worked together. The husband isn't particularly bright, and Yoshie's rather cautious. But I can't believe those two would frame their own Yūsaku.'

Kyōzō agreed with her.

'And finally, we have Mr. Saeki. What about him?'

Tamiko pondered for a while and then offered her opinion: 'He's quite smart, but not what I'd call clever or shrewd. What I mean is, he's good at studying. As for his personality… I'm sorry, I don't know him that well. But it would be all for the best if he did turn out to be the murderer….'

'And why so?'

'Because it would be awful if the murderer were someone in the family or someone dear to us, wouldn't it?' replied Tamiko, implying it was nothing more than common sense.

Kyōzō nodded, but in his mind, he thought Tamiko was the awful one here.

'I see your point. You've given me much food for thought. I think I'll leave it at that for today.'

Kyōzō stood up and was about to leave the room, when he looked at Yukie. Her pleading eyes left an impression in his mind.

You are the only one I can rely on.

He knew very well what she was signalling to him.

It was at that moment that he knew he had fallen in love.

This was the fiftieth time he had fallen in love, starting in third grade in elementary school. The forty-nine broken hearts he had suffered were all a prelude to meeting Yukie.

The number fifty invoked a sense of destiny.

He had a feeling that, this time, things would go well.

Of course, he had also forgotten that the very same feeling had been wrong forty-nine times in a row.

CHAPTER FOUR: SHINJI ADMITS TO BEING A REALIST

1

'There was another armed robbery today,' said the division chief, after calling Kyōzō to his office.

'I heard about it, sir.'

'You heard about it? You're acting as if you have nothing to do with it, while everybody else is wearing their shoe leather out looking for clues!?'

'I didn't mean....'

The chief gave a deep sigh and picked up a document from his desk.

'Okuda from the S Police Station filed a complaint. He says he had to let the suspect go because you were sticking your nose in places which were none of your business.'

'It's a misunderstanding, sir! The suspect's innocent, so of course Okuda had to let him go.'

'Innocent, you say? Based on this report, I have great trouble understanding how you arrived at that conclusion. Care to explain yourself?'

'Well, yes, how should I put it...There are a few points that don't make sense if he's the murderer—.'

The chief sighed again, and cut Kyōzō off.

'Inspector. Let's get this over with quickly. According to this report, Yūsaku Yano's the only person who could have committed the crime. Is that correct?'

Kyōzō wetted his lips and replied nervously: 'It does appear that way....'

'But you think they're wrong?' pressed the chief.

'Perhaps they are wrong... Because I don't believe Yūsaku did it.'

'Inspector! You need to face the facts! Gut feeling is important to a police detective, but you cannot rely solely on your gut feeling if it means ignoring the plain truth!'

'You're absolutely right of course, but—.'

'You simply won't learn. It's unlike you, you know. Anyway, this case goes to S Police Station. You're assigned to the armed robberies as of today.'

Kyōzō panicked.

'Please wait, sir! I'm just about to get my hands on something substantial! There's something strange about this case. I'm sure there's more to it than meets the eye.'

'The whole world is full of strange happenings.' The chief shrugged off Kyōzō's protests.

'Chief!'

The chief turned his chair around so his back was facing Kyōzō and stared out of the window. After a short silence he continued, but there was a note of resignation in his tone.

'You seem very tired, Inspector. I never thought you were a coolheaded person, but you're really acting up today. I'm afraid I'll have to give you two days off to rest.'

Kyōzō didn't know what he was hearing. A few days off at this busy time? Was the chief suspending him?

'I am not tired at all, and I am always coolheaded. Please allow me to continue the investigation, sir.'

The chief clicked his tongue and turned his chair around to face Kyōzō again.

'You are a slow one, aren't you? I can't assign you to a case we've already handed over to the local police station without a good reason. That's why I'm giving you a couple of days off. And what you do in your own time is none of my business.'

Kyōzō finally understood what the chief was telling him. He had two days to dig something up.

'Thank you very much, chief. You're really the be—.'

'I have no idea what you're talking about. All I said was that you're of no use to us at the moment. Oh, and I think I should give Kinoshita some time off too.'

So Kinoshita would be available at the same time....

Kyōzō desperately fought back the urge to give the chief a kiss.

'Eh. So I have to work even though I got a few days off?' grumbled Kinoshita as he was preparing to leave the hospital. 'It's been a while, so I was planning to go on a date with Sanae....'

'You idiot! Who cares about your Sanae!? The only reason you got a few days off is because of the Chief's gentle heart, to put you on the Kikuichirō case with me!'

Kinoshita regarded Kyōzō with suspicion.

'But that's just your guess, isn't it, sir? I mean I'm a patient, remember? Why wouldn't he give me a few days off to recover?'

'Why wouldn't he? You know how busy it is right now. The Chief's not so kind-hearted he'd give a low-level detective like you time off just because of a sprained ankle.'

Seeing how eager Kyōzō was, Kinoshita raised his hands in defeat.

'Okay, I get it. But how are we going to investigate the case again?'

Kinoshita's question hit a sore spot.

'You know what they say: if necessary, we'll go over the crime scene a hundred times. It's the foundation of any crime investigation. Let's start from the beginning again.'

Kyōzō decided he'd keep silent about Yukie's latest testimony for the time being. It wasn't that he didn't believe her, but he also thought it unlikely that Setsuko was the murderer. In any case, Yūsaku would remain a suspect unless they managed to solve the mystery of his locked bedroom. Mentioning Yukie's testimony would do nothing to solve that mystery. It was clear, however, that they'd need to check up on Setsuko once again.

'Yo—you can't mean you want me to do that acrobatic stunt again...,' said Kinoshita, turning as white as a sheet.

Kyōzō thought about it for a second.

'No, you can forget about it. We'll leave that part out this time.'

The two detectives headed out once again for The 8 Mansion, but the only result they got there—and Kyōzō himself thought it made the case even messier—was Mitsuko Kawamura's confirmation of Yukie's earlier testimony, as she too declared that the murderer had been holding the crossbow on his left side.

2

'Oh, so this is your brother's coffee shop?'

'Yep.'

The two exhausted detectives had not found one shred of hope, so they had gone to Sunny Side Up for a free cup of coffee. The clock showed five o'clock in the afternoon and the shop was still open.

'Welco—oh, it's only you.'

The warm smile on Ichio's face vanished immediately.

'I'm exhausted. Hot coffees, two of them. This here is Kinoshita,' explained Kyōzō briskly. He sat down in his usual spot and indicated to Kinoshita to sit beside him.

'Yeah, yeah. Oh, by the way, Shin was waiting for you. He has something to tell you. Boss!'

Shinji's standing orders to Ichio were always to call him boss whenever there were customers present.

The boss appeared from a room in the back. He had apparently been taking a break.

'Oh, it's you. I've been reading the evening paper. He got released, I gather.'

'Yep,' replied Kyōzō, with a sour look on his face.

'So the investigation isn't over yet?'

Kyōzō glanced at Kinoshita for a second.

'The case has been handed over to S Police Station. The two of us have been given a few days off to work on the case unofficially.'

'How wonderful! Sacrificing your free days to save a young, innocent man! It's like one of those hot-blooded police television dramas!'

Ichio held a silver tray to her chest as she praised the two.

'Oh, then I suppose I'm too late,' muttered Shinji, looking serious.

'Have you thought of something?'

'Maybe. You see, I was a fool for thinking that trick with the clock could be pulled off. It's far too risky, as you'd get a two-hour difference from the actual time of death. So of course that idea was a non-starter.'

Kyōzō nodded.

'And we all overlooked one crucial point.'

'And that is...?'

'It was a premeditated murder,' said Shinji suggestively, but Kyōzō wasn't impressed.

'What makes you think that? And what difference does it make if it was?'

'The answer to your first question is simple. The crossbow was stolen one week ago—or at least, that's what Yūsaku told the others. If he's telling the truth, then that means the murder was planned at least a week beforehand. And the same holds even if Yūsaku does turn out to be the murderer after all.'

While she had phrased it differently, this was basically what Tamiko had said as well. Kyōzō had no objections to this line of reasoning.

Shinji took a deep breath, and then continued: 'So what are the implications of the murder being premeditated? The killer stole the crossbow one week ago, or else he—Yūsaku—lied about it being stolen then. And on the night of the murder, the killer used some means to lure Kikuichirō out into the connecting gallery and kill him there. But why? Why commit the murder inside the house? Had the murder been committed outside, there would have been more suspects. If the culprit had killed Kikuichirō in some dark alley without any obvious suspects around, the police would have had to consider the possibility of a random killing. But even though that would have been more convenient, the murderer still chose to commit the crime inside the house. And in front of two witnesses, no less. What's more—and this is important—the two witnesses were chatting, with the lights on. The lights in Yūsaku's room, on the other hand, were off. There would have been some moonlight illuminating the inner courtyard, but it still must have been quite dark. Do you really believe it's possible that the two witnesses could see the murderer, but he couldn't see them?'

'Of course he saw them. But only after he'd committed the crime. He was probably concentrating solely on Kikuichirō until he'd done what he'd set out to do,' said Kyōzō.

'Impossible. Think about it. The lights in all the other rooms were out, except for Yukie's room. Not noticing the lights is out of the question. Consider the murderer's psychology. He'd have been nervous about being seen by anybody. I'd think he'd be paying even more attention to the environment than to Kikuichirō. Remember, this was a premeditated murder. Kikuichirō was only there in the gallery at one in the morning because the killer had called him out there. But one o'clock in the night isn't all that strange a time to be still awake, is it? And then you have a room where the lights are still actually on. So why wasn't the crime committed at a later time? Why didn't the murderer wait until everybody was asleep? And to return to my earlier question, why commit the crime inside the house anyway?'

Kyōzō pondered the questions. He glanced at Kinoshita, who also seemed to be giving them some thought.

Kyōzō gave up.

'I have no idea. Why? You've obviously got an idea.'

Shinji grinned as he poured some more coffee for the two detectives. When he continued he spoke much more slowly.

'You see, when you first told me how the crime was committed, I was reminded of a certain novel....'

'There it is! Your trademark move: acting pretentiously.'

Ichio was the heckler of course, but Shinji did not react to her comment.

'I'm sure you've read it too, Ichio. It's *The Emperor's Snuff-Box*[vii]. The circumstances in that novel are very similar to this case. It starts with a couple discussing something in a room, when they happen to witness a murder being committed in the house across the street.'

Ichio appeared to recall the story as Shinji described it.

'Now you mention it, that does sound similar. But the trick used there wouldn't work here. Because—.'

Shinji cut her off quickly.

'Yes, I know. But I still thought there was something odd going on when I heard that the two witnesses had been attacked and knocked out for almost two hours. And the witnesses hadn't even cried out for help. Yukie obviously couldn't even have cried anyway, but what about Mitsuko Kawamura? Don't you think things turned out really conveniently for the murderer, despite him supposedly having attacked the two women in a panic?'

'I have no idea what you're trying to tell us. Do you, Kinoshita?'

'I don't see it either,' replied Kinoshita promptly. He had given up thinking.

'Shinji, just tell us what you're trying to say.'

Shinji sighed and complied with his brother's order.

'What I'm trying to say is that the culprit killed Kikuichirō knowing very well that there were two witnesses present.'

'What? He knew he was being seen? But then why would he still commit the murder?'

'To frame Yūsaku, of course.'

'Bu—but how did he enter Yūsaku's room?'

'That's the one thing I haven't worked out. At least, not so far.'

Kyōzō was disappointed by the answer. From the way Shinji had acted, he thought his younger brother had worked everything out.

'So what use is your oh-so-brilliant theory, then?'

Shinji looked as if he didn't know how to explain it more simply.

'You really don't see it? Why do you think the murderer knew there'd be witnesses?'

'Anybody would notice it if the curtains of a lit room are suddenly drawn open.'

Kyōzō hadn't noticed he was contradicting his own earlier words.

'That won't do. The murderer must have already known there would be two witnesses, when he summoned Kikuichirō into the covered gallery.'

'But he couldn't have known…' Kyōzō started to say, but then he opened his eyes wide as he looked at Shinji. He had finally grasped what his younger brother had been trying to tell him.

'An accomplice! Mitsuko Kawamura was in on it!' he shouted. But Shinji cocked his head slightly.

'We can't say for sure at the moment. The point is that, at one o'clock, either Mitsuko Kawamura or Yukie had to open the curtains. That doesn't mean that either one of them was involved deeply enough to be called an accomplice. I haven't seen the crime scene for myself, so I can't say for sure, but you said there was a carpet laid out in the gallery, didn't you? And they opened the curtains in Yukie's room supposedly because they'd heard someone walking in the gallery, yes? But could they realistically have heard footsteps walking out there from inside Yukie's room? I suspect the murderer made clever use of one of those two witnesses.'

'But… Yukie said that they heard someone coming, so Mitsuko opened the curtains to peek out. Which means both of them heard the footsteps….'

'That might be the case, but how about this? Suppose Mitsuko draws open the curtains and says she hears footsteps. And, lo and behold, Kikuichirō is indeed standing outside. It wouldn't be all that strange for Yukie to imagine she'd heard the footsteps herself in that case. A slight variant on what happens in *The Emperor's Snuff-Box*.'

'Oh wow, you sound just like Dr. Fell[viii]!'

Shinji blushed in response to Ichio's praise.

'*The Emperor's Snuff-Box* doesn't feature Dr. Fell, I'm sorry to say,' he replied, correcting her.

'Who was in it then? Not H.M….[ix]'

'Kinross. Dr. Kinross[x].'

'Who cares? Or wait, perhaps I should be grateful to those doctors because we made some progress. Kinoshita, let's go. Let's see what Mitsuko has to tell us.'

Kyōzō got up, with Kinoshita following suit, but Shinji quickly stopped them.

'I can't say for sure whether Mitsuko or Yukie were even aware they were helping the murderer. It's possible they were being used without their knowledge. So it might be difficult to get the answers you want. As long as the mystery of the locked room remains unsolved, I doubt you'll be able to solve the whole case.'

Kyōzō considered Shinji's warning for a moment, but then pointed a large finger at his brother.

'All right. You solve the locked room mystery and we'll focus on Mitsuko and Yukie. Okay?'

'What do you mean, solve the mystery?'

'You know I hate complicated stuff like that. But if you can't solve it, Ichio, you do it.'

Ichio's eyes sparkled.

'Oh, could I see the crime scene, then?'

'I'll ask Yukie... Only if she's all right with inviting you over.'

'Yes! I'll do my best!'

Ichio was thrilled being given such a rare chance.

Shinji, too, appeared resigned to his fate, and opened his hands wide.

'All right. I'll help out as well. But just to be clear, unlike you, brother, I don't believe in Yūsaku's innocence. All I did was make a deduction, just like the detectives in mystery novels, but I'm not sure it would fly in the real world, which is brimming with irrationality. Real people don't always act in a rational manner. People in the real world act on a whim, they do foolish things, they make mistakes. When something curious happens in a novel, that means there's something important behind it. But in the real world, it could be nothing but mere coincidence. People like Ichio and me, who have been corrupted by detective fiction, sometimes forget about that, and rely solely on logic. It appears you want Ichio and me to help on this case, so let me tell you straight: I—and probably Ichio too—we'd be delighted if it turns out Yūsaku is really innocent, and that some kind of trick was used to create a locked room. However, I am of the opinion Yūsaku is indeed the murderer. I hope you understand that's my honest conclusion.'

He stopped.

'Can you believe this guy! I never realised until now, Shin, that you haven't even an ounce of romanticism in your heart! I'll take back the praise I heaped on you just now. I think you're more like Inspector French[xi].'

That was all Ichio had to say.

'I see the point you're making, Shinji. But this case is fishy, no matter how you look at it. There's something not quite right about it. That's why I asked for your help. I need the special minds of both of you.'

'If you really want our help, I'm in. But don't expect too much from me.'

Kyōzō still had a bemused expression on his face as he went outside with Kinoshita. Thanks to Shinji's theory, he now knew that Mitsuko—or Yukie—was in possession of the key to solving this case, yet Shinji himself claimed he didn't believe his own theory. Was Yūsaku perhaps the murderer after all?

No, it couldn't be. Kyōzō considered himself to be too good a judge of character. Shinji might have his suspicions because he hadn't met Yūsaku in person yet, but there was no way Yūsaku was the murderer.

That was what Kyōzō told himself as he headed back to The 8 Mansion by car.

3

Seven o'clock in the evening. Upon their arrival at The 8 Mansion Kyōzō and Kinoshita discovered that the Yanos and Yūsaku had all returned. Even though Yūsaku was still a suspect, Tamiko had called them back to the house, saying: 'It might be a different story if he'd been convicted, but Yūsaku hasn't even been arrested, so there's no reason why you shouldn't return home.'

Kyōzō, however, suspected that Tamiko simply needed Yoshie there to keep the house running.

The two detectives waited in the parlour until the residents had finished dinner, after which Kyōzō started his questioning of Mitsuko in her room. What he would really have preferred was to take her with him as a material suspect, but that was out of the question at that point.

Kyōzō had Kinoshita remain in the hallway while he entered her room alone. He looked around in silence in order to put some unspoken pressure on her. Shinji had suggested that Mitsuko might have aided the murderer unwittingly, but considering she still hadn't said anything about such an event to the police, Kyōzō thought it was more likely she was an accomplice.

Her hobby appeared to be fabricating her own clothes, as there were a lot of dressmaking patterns and pieces of cloth lying around. On the desk were some scraps and a sewing machine with a key in it.

Given the modest size of her closet, she didn't seem to own many pieces of clothing, although next to the closet stood a large, full-length mirror which could capture the whole of Kyōzō's sizeable body, even up close.

Kyōzō continued to look around in silence. Eventually Mitsuko could bear it no longer and broke her silence:

'Please take a seat. Would you like something to drink?'

Kyōzō sat down, but declined the drink.

'This is your second visit today. Did you discover anything?'

Kyōzō tried to read her true intentions from her small talk, but there was nothing suspicious about her.

‘To be honest, yes. But I first I’d like to ask you about your statement again. At one o’clock in the morning, while you were in Yukie’s room, you heard footsteps along the covered gallery and opened the curtains, correct?’

‘…Did I say that? I think that Yukie opened the curtains.’

Kyōzō had tried to trap her on the footsteps, but she had shrugged it off.

‘But Yukie said that you opened the curtains.’

‘Did she? I suppose I must have done then. I don’t really remember. You must understand, considering what happened afterwards….’

There was nothing he could do about it if she claimed she couldn’t remember.

‘I see. Anyway, one of you opened the curtains. There you saw Mr. Kikuichirō. And someone killed him with a crossbow from Yūsaku’s room. Didn’t you scream, having witnessed all of that?’

‘…I suppose I might have screamed. Why?’

If this woman is indeed the accomplice, she’s also an accomplished liar, thought Kyōzō.

‘What I mean is that it’s highly unusual for a person to scream murder and then leave the safety of the room. It must take a lot of courage for a woman to leave the room of her own free will, knowing that there’s a murderer lurking outside.’

‘…But at that time we hadn’t really grasped yet what had happened. Did I say something strange? I don’t see the point you’re making.’

Kyōzō decided to put the matter to her straightforwardly.

‘No, I think you do see my point. What I want to know from you is… the name of the real murderer.’

For a moment a look of panic spread over her face, but it quickly disappeared to make place for the usual expression of feigned ignorance.

‘The murderer is… Yūsaku, isn’t it? What’s the meaning of this? Didn’t you say you had some routine questions to ask me? But it’s almost as if….’

‘No, I am not saying that you committed the murder. It would have been impossible for you, of course. But what I think is that you know who the real murderer is, and it’s not Yūsaku. Is it Setsuko? She’s the only other left-handed person in this house besides you and Yūsaku. Or did the murderer shoot from his left side on purpose, to frame Yūsaku?’

Kyōzō frowned at Mitsuko as he accused her, but she merely replied, with a perplexed expression: ‘I don’t know anything.’

Kyōzō was not absolutely convinced she was lying to him. But he had no other choice but to push forward.

'We already know the role you played in the murder. The only things we don't know are the name of the murderer, and how it was done. If you confess everything now, you'll be charged with something small, like covering up evidence. But if you remain stubborn like this, we'll have no choice but to....'

He shook his head as if in disappointment.

'And what precisely is it that you think I did? Please say it out loud!'

There was anger in her voice.

'...You were asked by someone to open the curtains at one o'clock on the night of the murder, pretending to have heard footsteps.'

Mitsuko laughed as if she had never heard such nonsense.

'And that's my crime?'

'So you admit it?'

'I might have opened the curtains. But nobody asked me to open them. What's the difference?'

'If nobody asked you, Ms. Kawamura, then why did you open them?' countered Kyōzō quickly.

'Because... I heard footsteps.'

It had taken a long time, but Kyōzō was relieved he had finally caused her to speak those words.

'Aha. If you could hear footsteps from Yukie's room, I assume the same holds for this room.'

'What do you mean?'

Kyōzō stood up and went over to the window.

'Can you hear any footsteps from the gallery now?'

Surprised, Mitsuko tried to listen for them. She looked at Kyōzō and said slowly: '...No, I don't hear any.'

'Quite right. I can't hear them either,' he said, as he suddenly drew the curtains open. Kinoshita, who had been walking up and down the covered gallery, came into view.

Kyōzō gave a sign and Kinoshita came over to Mitsuko's room, with a cheerful expression on his face.

'So? Was I of any help?' he asked expectantly, and Kyōzō nodded vigorously.

'Ms. Kawamura, I think you now understand. Neither you nor Yukie could have heard Kikuichirō walking down the gallery. That means you had to know beforehand that he'd be there at one o'clock.'

‘Why me? I didn’t say I opened the curtains. I only said I might have done. It was probably Yukie who opened them.’

‘She remembers clearly that it was you who opened them.’

Mitsuko appeared to have lost interest. ‘Then I suppose it will just have to be an endless argument.’

Kyōzō finally exploded.

‘I’ve had enough! Listen carefully. As I already told you, opening the curtains because someone asked you to isn’t a big crime on its own. But it’s a completely different story if you cooperated in the full knowledge that a murder was about to be committed. And that’s what I think happened. Someone asked you to hang around in Yukie’s room until one, and to open the curtains at that precise moment. That’s when you witnessed the murder and realised that same person was the killer, but you became afraid and didn’t tell the police about it. Am I right? Or were you in on the murder scheme right from the start?’

Mitsuko looked as if she had had quite enough and stood up.

‘I think it would be quite meaningless to continue this discussion. I didn’t lie, and no matter how much you threaten me, I can’t tell you about things I don’t know. And, supposing someone else besides Yūsaku is the murderer, how did they get inside his room?’

Kyōzō had no answer for her. Just as Shinji had said, as long as they didn’t solve the locked room mystery, he wouldn’t be able to wrap up the case.

‘Could you please leave?’

Kyōzō got up slowly and, as he was about to leave, turned around to glare at Mitsuko. It was the look he had used to make gangsters tremble, back when he was in Division 4.

‘We have our eyes on you. You’d better be careful not to make any mistakes from now on.’

And with that warning he left the room.

Kinoshita tried to do the same and glared at Mitsuko, but she glared back, and he quickly fled for the door.

Just at that moment an unfortunate accident happened.

The door Kyōzō had slammed shut in his temper broke Kinoshita’s nose.

Two weeks for full recovery.

4

Kinoshita was carried into the empty guest room two doors away and a doctor was called.

As he was waiting for the doctor to finish, Kyōzō had an idea.

He could use this accident!

Mitsuko Kawamura was without a doubt on edge now, knowing that she was under suspicion. It was quite possible she might take some action sometime during the night. If they could stay in the house to watch her, she might make a mistake, or cave under the mental pressure and give herself up.

'Doctor, there's something I want to ask of you.'

'Yes?'

'Could you perhaps tell the others it would be better for Kinoshita to stay here for the night?'

The doctor looked puzzled.

'I don't mind, but may I ask why?'

Kyōzō pulled his police notebook from his pocket and showed it to the doctor.

'I can't explain the details, but it's necessary for my investigation,' he replied.

'But I thought they'd already caught the culprit?' said the doctor. Kyōzō looked around to make sure nobody was listening and whispered: 'We did that to put the real murderer at ease.'

The doctor looked bewildered for a second, but then a big smile spread across his face.

'Oh! That means....'

'Shh... You understand, don't you? Please don't mention this to anyone until we nab the real killer.'

'Ye—yes, of course. You might be surprised how good I am at keeping a secret. I see, so he wasn't the real murderer. The wife will be so surprised when she hears this. Oh, but mum's the word. The police do play a crafty game....'

'So I hope you can help me out here.'

'Of course. It's the duty of the people to help the police in their investigations.'

Kyōzō didn't trust people who could utter the words "duty of the people" without any embarrassment, but he had no other choice.

The two of them went downstairs. There were several people waiting for them on the ground floor. The only persons absent were the secretary Saeki, the master of the house Kikuo, and Yūsaku, who had remained in his room all the time.

'...How is that poor boy?' asked Tamiko anxiously, whilst Kikuji grinned. The doctor stole a glance at Kyōzō, and explained: 'He broke his nose. That's a fairly routine condition, so it's nothing to worry about. However, there's a possibility he hit his head hard, so I've advised that he not be moved tonight.'

Kyōzō was satisfied with this likely-sounding lie.

'I see. I suppose it can't be helped. He can stay in that guest room tonight, then. I hope that's all right?'

So, before Kyōzō could suggest it himself, Tamiko had already offered the room.

'Yes. I'm terribly sorry for causing you so much trouble. I'm quite worried about him, so I think I'll stay by his side tonight as well.'

'I see. I'll have a guest room in the south wing readied for you, so you can use it if you want to rest.'

'Thank you very much.'

Kyōzō grinned to himself. He shot a glance at Mitsuko, but she looked away, pretending she'd had nothing to do with it.

5

'Uuugh… I—Inspector….'

'Oh, finally awake, Kinoshita?'

But his colleague had not in fact awakened. Kinoshita was still lying on the bed, his eyes closed.

'….I knew I'd die one day working for that man… I shouldn't have come to Tōkyō… Mom, I'm sorry I'll go to the other side first….'

Kyōzō clicked his tongue, got up and shook his colleague.

'Kinoshita! You there?!'

The latter's eyelids twitched and then opened.

'Where am I?' he mumbled as he looked around the room.

'In the Hachisuka house. We'll be staying here tonight.'

Kyōzō helped Kinoshita as he tried painfully to sit up.

'Oh, ouch. That means I'm not…?'

'Don't worry, you're still among the living. You only broke your nose.'

'I only broke my nose? Good to hear tha—that's not good!'

He carefully moved his hand to his nose, and touched the gauze there.

'Oh no! What if my face ends up like yours? Aah, Sanae won't like me anymore….'

'It'll look fine, maybe your face will finally look more like a real police detective then… What did you just say? What's wrong with my face? My nose isn't broken!'

‘I simply misspoke. …You see, I’m not smart, and I’m not strong either. All I have is my face…,’ said Kinoshita humbly, and he started to wail.

‘Oh, I’ve had enough! I’m going to patrol around the house. I’ll leave the door and curtains open, so you can also keep an eye out from here.’

‘Keep an eye out? For what?’

‘Mitsuko Kawamura of course. She will definitely try to contact the murderer tonight to discuss what to do next. She might have been acting tough, but inside she was trembling.’

‘But would she really attempt something as dangerous as that while we’re still here in the house?’

Kinoshita wiped his eyes. He appeared to have calmed down.

‘I can’t say. She might be patient and hold out for one more night, which would be our loss. But for the moment, tonight’s our only chance.’

Kyōzō opened the curtains and window wide open and stared up at the night sky. It was cloudy, so the moon and stars were not visible. Something hung in the air, as if a storm was brewing. He remembered the weather forecast on the radio had said it might rain in the night.

Something was about to happen.

Kyōzō tried to dismiss the feeling from his mind.

CHAPTER FIVE: KYŌZŌ RECALLS A HIGH SCHOOL LESSON

1

Eleven o'clock in the evening. Kyōzō noticed that the light in Yukie's room was still on, so although he feared the hour might be too late, he decided to knock on her door.

'Miss Yukie, are you still up?'

The face that appeared from behind the door looked more sorrowful with every passing day, but despite that she had not lost one bit of her beauty. The sight of her stabbed Kyōzō in the heart.

…I want to protect you.

Kyōzō almost mumbled the lyrics from a Yuming song[xii].

'There was something I wanted to ask you.'

Her fragile smile seemed to ask what was the matter.

'Do you remember my brother and sister, who were in the coffee shop? I'd like you to invite them here to the house. The two of them are big fans of mystery fiction… No, they aren't just curious to see a murder scene. You see, they are much cleverer than I am, and I asked them to help me out with my investigation. Could you invite them over tomorrow as your friends and allow them to take a look around the house, just for one day?'

Yukie looked doubtful and started moving her hands, but then she remembered that Kyōzō didn't understand sign language, and left him to get her word processor.

Kyōzō was deep in thought as he waited for her in the doorway. He should learn sign language. It was both troublesome and time-consuming for her to get her word processor every time they needed to talk. And perhaps, in the future, they would….

Yukie returned and expertly started typing with her right hand, while holding the word processor up in her left.

'*I don't mind, but I know almost nobody besides my family and the other people in the house. I don't think anyone would believe they're my friends.*'

'Well, we aren't trying to deceive anybody. I think it'll be all right as long as they're properly invited here. It's just that I can't get them over here through formal police channels.'

'Then I'll be happy to help out.'

'Thank you. I think we're starting to find our way through the fog. There's another thing I want to ask you. Are you sure it was Mitsuko Kawamura who opened the curtains on the night of the murder, and not you?'

Yukie didn't understand the significance of the question, but nodded by way of agreement anyway.

Kyōzō hadn't had any confirmation that Mitsuko had lied to him until that moment.

'All right, that clears things up. Please cheer up. I'll definitely find the murderer tomorrow.'

Kyōzō felt himself growing braver in front of Yukie.

2

Midnight. Kyōzō was wandering around the second floor, keeping an ear out for the noise of the occasional door opening and closing. He had a good idea of where the people in the house were. Was Kinoshita also keeping an eye as ordered?

Saeki and the master of the house, Kikuo, were in Kikuo's study, busy with the work Kikuichirō had left behind. Even Kikuo couldn't manage all of that by himself.

All the other residents were presumably in their rooms.

While Kyōzō was restlessly pacing up and down the west hallway, he heard a door open in the north wing. He made his way quickly to the source of the noise, and found Mitsuko, who had just come out from her room. She held a key in her hand.

'What's the matter?' he asked, and she shot him a spiteful look.

'I was thinking of having something to drink before going to bed. Did you think I was going to kill someone?'

Kyōzō knew that her irritated tone betrayed the agitation she was feeling.

'I'm feeling a bit thirsty myself, actually. Let's go together.'

He followed Mitsuko downstairs to the ground floor and they entered the kitchen. She took a bottle of milk out of the refrigerator and started to make a cup of hot cocoa. Kyōzō took a glass from the cupboard and poured some milk for himself. He quietly watched Mitsuko as he slowly drank it. The hand that was busy stirring the pan was trembling.

After a few minutes, she could no longer bear his watching eyes, and turned rround with a scowl on her face.

Kyōzō braced himself for an explosion, but instead she asked quietly: 'Are you watching me?'

'Oh, you noticed? You're quite observant,' he replied sarcastically.

'It's sad to see my tax money go to waste like this,' Mitsuko said cynically.

She poured the hot cocoa into a cup and went back up to her room, without a second look at the detective on her trail. After watching Mitsuko unlock the door with her key and disappear inside her room, Kyōzō resumed his patrol.

And then it was one o'clock....

And the second tragedy happened.

3

Bang.

There was a loud slamming noise and the sound of a woman shrieking.

It was followed by the sound of doors opening here and there in the house, and people calling out to each other.

Kyōzō swiftly determined that the cry had originated from Mitsuko's room and ran the short distance at full speed.

When he arrived at her door, he saw that Kinoshita had come out of his room, wondering what had happened.

'Sir! What was that?'

Kyōzō didn't reply, but knocked loudly on Mitsuko's door.

'Ms. Kawamura! What's the matter?!' he cried as he rattled the doorknob. The door appeared to be locked.

'Ms. Kawamura!'

There was no reply.

There was a sudden flash of light, followed by another scream. It came from another room.

What was going on? And what was that flash of light? Such thoughts flew through Kyōzō's mind as he heard the rumbling of thunder. He turned around in surprise and looked out through the window. The rain suddenly came pouring down.

Yūsaku opened his door and came out into the hallway with a drowsy expression on his face, calling out to Kyōzō:

'What's happened?'

'I don't know!'

Yukie came running too, wearing a night gown over her negligée.

Diagram 2

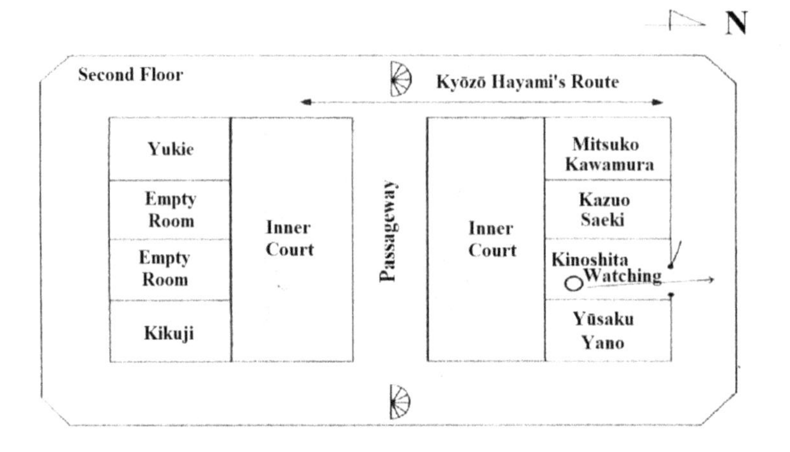
N
Second Floor
Kyōzō Hayami's Route
Yukie
Empty Room
Empty Room
Kikuji
Inner Court
Passageway
Inner Court
Mitsuko Kawamura
Kazuo Saeki
Kinoshita
Watching
Yūsaku Yano

Kikuji was behind her, dressed similarly—not in a negligée of course.

'Did something happen?' he asked Kyōzō, as if it was his doing.

'I'm not sure. I think something happened in Ms. Kawamura's room. Mr. Kikuji, could you fetch the key to this room please?'

Kikuji grumblingly made his way downstairs. As he left, an alarmed Saeki joined the group as well.

'Inspector! It's Mrs. Hachisuka....'

'You mean Mrs. Tamiko? What's the matter?'

Kyōzō suspected that the second scream had come from her. What had happened to her?

'She's... she's rather agitated....'

He appeared to be at a loss for words.

'But she wasn't hurt in any way, was she? She's not wounded or anything?'

'No, she isn't. She says she saw... a crossbow.'

'The crossbow? She found the crossbow? Where is it?'

Kyōzō appeared startled, but Saeki shook his head.

'She didn't find it. According to her, it was aimed at her from outside the window.'

'Outside the window? You mean from the other side of the window? But her bedroom is on the first floor. And who was taking aim at her?'

'I didn't ask for the details actually, but I thought you should be notified at once, so I came running here,' he explained with some regret in his voice.

'And where is she now?'

'She's with the president.'

Tamiko appeared to be in no harm at that moment. The more pressing worry on his mind was Mitsuko.

'Could you please join them then? And I'd appreciate it if you could check up on Mrs. Setsuko too.'

Kyōzō didn't know for sure that something had happened, but it couldn't hurt to know exactly where everybody was.

Saeki nodded and quickly left. It was at that moment that Kikuji returned, dragging along Takao Yano, who was holding grimly onto his bunch of keys.

'What's the matter?'

Kyōzō was getting quite sick of being asked the same question over and over again, and merely shook his head.

'Give me the keys,' he ordered. Takao had no choice but to do so.

Kyōzō tried them one by one, and finally unlocked the door with the fourth key.

He pulled on the door, but it wouldn't budge, as if it had become unduly heavy. It was then that Kyōzō was taken aback by a metallic smell reaching his nose.

It was the smell of blood.

Yūsaku and Yukie anxiously exchanged glances.

'Inspector! Look down there, something's seeping through the carpet.'

As Kinoshita had pointed out, something wet was indeed seeping through.

Kyōzō pulled with all his strength and the door finally opened.

A flash of lightning illuminated the horrified expression on Mitsuko Kawamura's face, causing everyone present to cry out.

Mitsuko's body had been nailed to the weighty door. She was dressed in pyjamas that were drenched in blood at the front. The whole scene resembled something from a haunted house attraction. A metallic arrow had pierced her through the heart and was buried deep into the wood of the door.

'What the...,' gasped Kyōzō, immediately followed by a scream—or, more accurately, a noise—coming out of Yukie's throat, whereupon she fainted.

Fortunately, Kyōzō managed to grab hold of her before she fell to the floor.

'Please take her to her room! Everyone, please step away from the door! And contact the S Police Station. Damn it! Why....'

Kyōzō's sharp eyes scanned the room as he gave his orders. The window was open, and the curtains were swaying in the wind.

Heavy rain was coming in through the window. There was no sign of Mitsuko's murderer inside.

Had he escaped through the window?

Kyōzō was careful not to step in the pool of blood as he cautiously entered the room, bracing himself for any sudden surprise. He went over to the window, stuck his head out and looked all around, but there was nothing there out of the ordinary.

If the murderer hadn't escaped through the window... Kyōzō turned back to the room.

There was only one place a person could hide: the bathroom.

He put on the white gloves he always carried with him, inched silently towards the bathroom door, and flung it open suddenly.

Empty. He went in and peered into the bath tub. Reflexively, he even raised the lid of the toilet to look inside, but—not surprisingly—the murderer was not lurking there.

Baffled, Kyōzō mumbled to himself: 'But how....'

'Is... is anybody there?' asked Kinoshita from outside the room.

'No... Kinoshita, you were watching the hallway all the time, weren't you?'

'Of course. Nobody passed by my room.'

'...Does that mean the murderer entered and left through the window?'

Kyōzō thought about what had happened.

Damn. It was as if the murderer could fly around freely anywhere in the house. What on earth was going on?

4

'Mrs. Tamiko, I hope you feel better now.'

They were in Kikuo and Tamiko's bedroom. Tamiko was sitting next to her husband on the bed, drinking tea with a splash of brandy. Kyōzō had instructed Saeki and Kinoshita to wait outside while he questioned them.

'Yes... I'm all right now. Please ask us what you need to know.'

'I was told you saw the crossbow outside your window....'

'Yes, I was awakened by the scream—it must have been Mitsuko I heard. I looked out of the window and suddenly lightning struck.'

Kyōzō recalled there had been a flash of lightning just after Mitsuko's scream.

'It's then that I... the crossbow... yes, yes. I know it very well. The one Yūsaku had. The thing was outside the window, aiming at me. So I started to yell....'

Kyōzō felt slightly relieved now he knew that even Tamiko could feel fear, but he had to reconsider after hearing what Tamiko had to say next.

'I wondered why... but the only thing I've been afraid of ever since I was a child was lightning....'

Taken aback by her cool-headedness, Kyōzō took some time to formulate his next question.

'Well, yes... who was aiming at you? Did you see their face?'

'No, there was nobody there, only the crossbow.'

'Eh? What do you mean by "only the crossbow"?'

'The only thing floating outside the window was that crossbow, aimed at me,' said Tamiko nonchalantly, as she finished her tea.

Kyōzō wondered how he should interpret what he was being told.

Had a crossbow gone off flying on its own to kill Mitsuko? Her murderer had indeed seemed to disappear through a window on the second floor. That would be impossible unless the culprit could fly, but a single crossbow might be able to fly on its own, considering the weight....

Kyōzō dismissed such foolish ideas from his mind and asked:

'What happened next?'

'The thing was aiming at me, so I fled from the room, of course. And then Mr. Saeki came running.... He said he'd check and went into the room.'

'And then?' urged Kyōzō, even though Saeki had already told him that he hadn't found the crossbow.

'...There was nothing. The crossbow must have fled as well.'

Kyōzō wanted to point out that a crossbow couldn't flee, but he bit his tongue. Tamiko had probably had a nightmare, or mistaken something else for a crossbow, given that she was still half asleep at the time.

At that moment loud sirens could be heard in front of the house. At a quarter to two in the morning, Detective-Sergeant Okuda and his fellow police officers of S Police Station arrived, soon to be followed by the forensic unit of the Metropolitan Police Department, after which the real police investigation began.

The moment Okuda laid eyes on Kyōzō and Kinoshita, he asked: 'What's going on? Why are the two of you here?'

'We were convinced that Mitsuko Kawamura was in the possession of crucial information related to Kikuichirō's murder. So we put a bit of pressure on her... and now she's been murdered. We can assume that she was killed because the real murderer of Kikuichirō wanted to silence her. That means that Yūsaku's innocent.'

'I wonder. Tonight's murderer might be Yūsaku too, you know,' Okuda said, in a suspicious tone.

'You're wrong there. It only took me a few seconds to reach the crime scene after hearing the scream. Ten seconds at most. Do you think it would be possible for him to have climbed out of the window of Mitsuko's room and returned to his own room in a mere ten seconds? It would have been equally impossible for Yukie and Kikuji to commit this murder either, for the same reason.'

‘Hmm, we’ll accept that for the moment. But how could the murderer have entered and left through a room on the second floor? Perhaps they came from the roof, climbing down a rope?’

‘Ah, the roof, that’s an idea.’

As Kyōzō considered Okuda’s suggestion, he looked thoughtfully at Kinoshita.

Kinoshita detected Kyōzō’s look, and turned as white as a sheet.

‘No, Inspector, I definitely won’t do it.’

‘Did I say anything?’ replied Kyōzō, feigning ignorance.

‘That look… It’s that same look in your eye. You want me to do it again. I’ll tell you this, sir, I’m a patient. I’m still reco—.’

‘But I haven’t sai—.’

‘NOOOO WAAAAY! I know you want me to go up there. I know from painful experience how your mind works. You’re going to tell me that I’m better equipped for climbing down from the roof because I’m lighter, isn’t that right?’

‘You understand me so well. And yes, that’s exactly it. So, go climb down from the roof.’

Kinoshita was flabbergasted.

‘I’ve already told you! I’m out! There are a couple of men from the S Police Station here, I bet there’s a lightly-built person among them.’

‘Oh, so you want me to ask them? “Sorry, Kinoshita here is chicken, so could one of you go in his place?” You fool! Don’t forget that you’re a detective of Division 1 of the Metropolitan Police Department! Have no fear, it’ll go perfectly this time. With Okuda here and me supporting the rope, what could possibly go wrong?’

Kinoshita tried to plead for help from Okuda, but the other only nodded.

‘Okay, let’s get a rope. Where can we find one?’ ordered Kyōzō, leaving no further room for discussion.

‘I have a bad feeling about this. This time, I might really….’

‘Nonsense. I’m telling you, you’ll be all right.’

As Kinoshita left the room to look for a rope, he could be heard muttering: ‘I have a really, really bad feeling about this….’

5

Two-thirty in the morning. Kinoshita was standing on the roof above Mitsuko Kawamura’s room with a rope tied around his waist.

Several electric torches had been brought up to the roof by police officers, so it was quite bright around him, despite the time of night.

Although the rain had weakened, there was still a gentle drizzle, and nobody present could stop shivering.

'Please tie me up tightly. ...Doesn't this rope look dirty to you? It might be old. Won't it snap?'

'Stop yammering. It's not as if I'm asking you to climb a rock wall. You're just climbing down one or two metres. The rope won't snap.'

One end of the rope was tied around Kinoshita, and the other end Kyōzō had tied around himself. Another free part of the rope was tied around Okuda's waist. Their combined weight was close to two hundred kilograms. Kinoshita on the other hand weighed a mere sixty kilograms.

'Go!' ordered Kyōzō. Kinoshita started lowering the lower half of his body over the edge of the roof so it hung in the air.

When most of his body was over the edge, he grasped the rope firmly with both hands and supported himself by pushing his feet against the wall. Kyōzō felt the sudden force pulling on the rope, but it was a weight he could support with one single arm.

Step by step, Kinoshita started climbing down the wall. Or, to put it more precisely: Kinoshita was slowly lowered as Kyōzō and Okuda let out more rope.

It didn't take long for Kinoshita's feet to find the window sill of Mitsuko's room, diminishing the stress on the rope.

'I'm there! That's enough rope!'

Two police officers were standing inside the room, ready to pull him inside in the event that he slipped.

'So? Do you think you could fire a crossbow from there?'

'Hmm, yes, I do. What I think happened is that Ms. Kawamura saw the murderer outside the window and tried to run for the door. That's how she ended up nailed to it.'

The successful completion of his acrobatic act seemed to have put Kinoshita at ease, as he explained his own thoughts on the case for a change.

'That's probably what happened. Okay, we're done.'

Kyōzō and Okuda had already untied the ropes around their waists. They had naturally assumed that Kinoshita would simply climb inside Mitsuko's room.

But the now self-confident Kinoshita was of another mind. What would be more natural than leaving the same way he had come? So he dashingly started to climb back up the rope....

It goes without saying that the rope gave way the moment Kinoshita tried to climb up and entrusted his whole weight to it. The police officers inside were on the point of leaving the room, too, now their task had ended.

Kyōzō and Okuda saw the rope being pulled down, but thought Kinoshita was simply retrieving it.

The cry came the moment the end of the rope dropped off the roof.

'I knew it! I had a bad feeliiiiiiiiii—!'

Kyōzō realised Kinoshita was falling because he noticed the pitch of his cry was becoming lower due to the Doppler effect.

Sometimes even a boring physics class comes in handy, he thought.

Bam.

No, on second thoughts, maybe not.

Kinoshita had to be hospitalised with all four of his limbs broken.

6

The police finished questioning the witnesses at dawn, after which they moved over to the joint investigation headquarters for the case, which had been set up inside the S Police Station.

No reinforcements had come from the MPD. The section chief's reply was that Kyōzō would have to cope on his own, at least for that day. All the other officers were out.

While it was officially a joint investigation between the S Police Station and the MPD, Kyōzō was basically just an onlooker of the S Station investigation.

The man in command was Chief Inspector Kazumasa Tamura, who seemed eager to head a serial killer investigation. Well into his forties, he had no facial hair, unlike many of his contemporaries, which for some reason left a good impression on Kyōzō.

Tamura addressed the assembled detectives, coughed once and announced in a firm voice: 'Due to this latest murder, it's become necessary to reinvestigate the murder of Kikuichirō Hachisuka which occurred on the thirtieth of last month. We have no reinforcements from the MPD, but fortunately Police Inspector Hayami, who also worked on the first murder, will be here to support us in our investigation. Over to you, Okuda.'

Detective-Sergeant Okuda took over from the Chief Inspector and started by explaining the Kikuichirō murder.

'Everybody should have been handed a copy of the files by now, so I'll keep it short. We received a report on October 30th, at three a.m. that a murder had occurred in the Hachisuka residence. According to Yukie Hachisuka, and Mitsuko Kawamura, who had both witnessed the murder, the crime had happened at one o'clock. Their call to us had been delayed because after they had witnessed the murder, they had both been knocked out by someone we assume was the killer. He or she—let's assume it's a he, for the sake of argument—had used a crossbow to shoot Kikuichirō from the room of Yūsaku, son of the servants. Because it appeared that nobody besides Yūsaku could have entered his room that night, Police Inspector Hayami and I had Yūsaku brought in as a material witness. However, we were not able to arrest him due to lack of evidence. The murder weapon was also not discovered inside the house. We will have to wait for a report from Forensics before we can say definitely whether the crossbow used this time is the same as the one used in the Kikuichirō murder.'

Kyōzō got up slowly and stepped forward.

'I'm Hayami from the MPD. Before we move on to the Mitsuko Kawamura murder, I think it would be best if I explain my own thoughts on the Kikuichirō murder. I began to have doubts after talking to young Yūsaku Yano. If he were indeed the murderer, it would mean that he'd killed Kikuichirō from his own room, with his own crossbow, and that he had knocked the two witnesses, Mitsuko Kawamura and Yukie Hachisuka, out afterwards. But he also testified he'd been sleeping inside his room with the door locked. I can't believe that any murderer, knowing very well that there were two witnesses present, would say that. As you'll see in the files, at first sight it appears it's impossible for anyone to have made their way into his locked room, which is why I think some kind of trick was used. I'm of the opinion someone is trying to frame Yūsaku. But in order to do that, the culprit needed witnesses to the murder in the form of Mitsuko and Yukie. I concluded that Mitsuko must have been an accomplice to Kikuichirō's murder. Last night, detective Kinoshita and I questioned her. She didn't give anything away, but it was clear she was lying.'

'Inspector, could you please stick to the facts?' interjected Okuda irritably.

Kyōzō scowled at Okuda, but continued:

'...Anyway, Kinoshita and I remained in the house to observe Mitsuko. I was convinced she would try to contact the real murderer. She'd had no chance to speak to the killer face-to-face, so she probably used the telephone in her room to do so. The murderer panicked and killed her to prevent her from spilling the beans.'

'Pure speculation,' protested Okuda once again.

‘So do you have your own view of the case?’ asked Chief Inspector Tamura.

‘Of course. Only Yūsaku could have committed the first murder. Mitsuko Kawamura was one of the witnesses. And there’s nothing unusual about him wanting to kill a witness.’

‘Are you stupid!?’ exclaimed Kyōzō. ‘We already have Mitsuko’s testimony on paper, what use would it do to kill her now? Besides that, Yūsaku was inside his own room when I arrived at the crime scene. He couldn’t have climbed up to the roof and made it back into his room within the time frame.’

‘Just a moment. What’s this business about a roof?’ asked Tamura, who was having trouble following what was going on.

‘Sir, it’s clear from the circumstances that the murderer entered and left through the window. The crime scene is on the second floor, so the murderer probably used a rope or something similar to climb down from the roof into the victim’s room, and get away again,’ explained Kyōzō briefly, but Tamura frowned.

‘I see. From the roof. Even though you were in the west hallway? It not only seems dangerous, it seems completely reckless, to be frank.’

‘Reckless, sir? What do you mean?’ asked Kyōzō.

‘As long as you were patrolling in that hallway, there was a very significant possibility you would spot him. Why on earth take such a risk?’

Kyōzō had no answer.

‘But there isn’t any other way, so….’

‘Are you sure? Couldn’t the killer have shot the crossbow from the roof for example?’

‘Huh? But the victim was not even near the window.’

‘I’m talking about this roof.’

Tamura was pointing at the diagram of the house that was in the files. His finger was on the covered gallery.

‘If someone was lying here on the roof of the gallery, they wouldn’t need to worry about you seeing them, and they would have had a clear shot at Mitsuko in her room.’

It was a splendid suggestion. Kyōzō was impressed by Tamura’s reasoning. The man didn’t hold the title of Chief Inspector for nothing.

‘Excuse me, may I say something?’ asked one of the detectives timidly when the three senior detectives paused. ‘It’s about the roof.’

‘What about the roof?’ asked Tamura irritably.

The detective seemed to be hesitating whether to tell them or not, but quickly continued when he noticed the look on Tamura’s face.

'The door to the roof was locked. And there were no signs of it having been forced open without a key.'

Kyōzō remembered that he himself had opened the door to the roof with the bunch of keys he'd obtained from Takao.

'That's it! Takao Yano is in charge of all the keys!'

'So you think that's who did it? I remember he was in possession of the keys in the first murder as well.'

'Yes, but he had a solid alibi for the Kikuichirō murder, and his wife Yoshie stated she was with him during the second murder.'

It was then that Kyōzō started considering the possibility of the Yano couple as conspirators. It would all make sense then. Takao could have handed a copy of the room key to Yoshie. But it didn't seem likely the two of them would try to frame their own son. And if the two of them had worked together to kill Kikuichirō, then there'd be no reason for them to murder Mitsuko....

'The testimony of his wife, all by itself, is rather weak,' said Tamura. 'Anyway, we need to take a careful look at Takao and Yoshie, in relation to the Kikuichirō murder as well. And I want you to work even harder on finding the murder weapon. It's different with the first murder, but this time we know for sure that the murderer had no chance to smuggle the weapon out of the house. Go through every inch of the house and grounds and, no matter what, find that thing as soon as possible. This meeting is over,' he concluded.

Kyōzō was exhausted and decided to take forty winks at home first.

The circumstances had changed again by the time he was awakened by Shinji's afternoon phone call.

'Oh, you're home? Weren't we going to The 8 Mansion today? I even closed up the shop,' asked Shinji cheerfully.

'Hmmm? Oh yeah. What time is it?'

Kyōzō was still tired. Despite his efforts to get up, he fell back down immediately.

'Errr, about two? Were you sleeping?'

'Yeah, yesterday, or this morning rather, was horrible.'

'The murder of Mitsuko?'

'You know already? Well then, you know today is out of the question. Things have changed.'

'They have? But you know people will laugh at the police if you don't solve the case quickly. They'll criticise you for not stopping a serial killer....'

'Are you trying to threaten me?'

Shinji continued, paying his brother no attention: 'I heard Mitsuko's murder was also peculiar. Something about nobody could have done it. Give me the details.'

'Oh, what you don't know is we concluded that either of the Yano couple could've killed Mitsuko from the roof....'

There was silence for a moment.

'I guess you haven't heard yet? I don't know the details, but they are making lots of noise on television about it being an impossible murder.'

Kyōzō sat up immediately at the news. He was wide awake now.

'What did you say?'

'They were saying on television how it almost seemed like a flying human bee must have committed the murder. Apparently, forensics proved that the crossbow had been fired from above the inner courtyard.'

Something else for Kyōzō to worry about.

They hadn't solved Kikuichirō's murder yet, and already they had another impossible murder on their hands?

Shinji wasn't finished: 'Ichio, though, says it's just child's play....'

'What does she mean?'

'...I'll get Ichio for you. Ask her yourself.'

There was a moment's noise on the other side of the line, and then Ichio came on.

'You promised you'd take us to the mansion today! I even cancelled a date I had. Just because circumstances have changed doesn't mean you can all forget about it.'

'Have you really solved the mystery? The Mitsuko murder?'

'Well yes. I'm still working on the Kikuichirō murder, though.'

'But you don't even know exactly what happened.... I don't believe you. How did you solve it?'

Kyōzō was dubious, but he still made sure to listen carefully.

'...I'll explain later. I'll tell you inside The 8 Mansion. We'll be waiting in front of the gate at three. See you.'

'Hey, wait, I told you today's—.'

She had hung up.

Kyōzō remained rooted for a moment, lost in thought, but then quickly got out of bed, opened the blinds and switched on the television.

As Shinji had said, all channels were making a big fuss about the two murders that had happened in The 8 Mansion. A young male newscaster was rapidly explaining the circumstances under which

Diagram 3

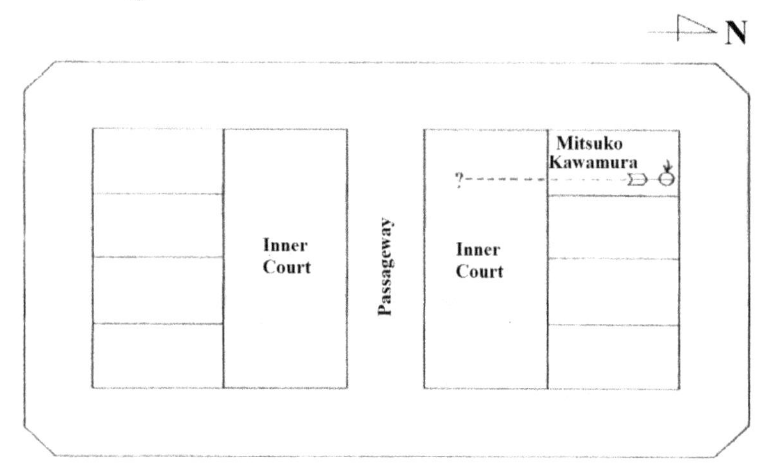

Mitsuko had been murdered, accompanied by footage of the firmly closed front gate and a floorplan of the premises.

'...According to Inspector Hayami Kyōzō of the Metropolitan Police Department who discovered the crime—.'

Kyōzō was about to cry for joy for getting mentioned and even getting his recent promotion right.

'—The victim, Ms. Mitsuko Kawamura, had been nailed to the door like "a statue of the Virgin Mary"...'

Kyōzō wondered whether he had in fact said such a thing, but then he realised how the metaphor was fundamentally wrong.

'Fools! The Virgin Mary has nothing to do with it! I never said anything like that!' he yelled, as he threw his pillow at the television. The newscaster, however, had not noticed the mistake and continued: 'But what makes this case especially mystifying is the following, isn't it, Midori?'

'Yes,' replied the female newscaster dressed in traditional Japanese clothing.

'According to the police, the crossbow used in the murder had been fired at an almost horizontal level, from a distance of five or six metres.'

'Yes.'

'But can you believe it!? Take a look at this floorplan. As you can see here, there's nothing at all at the place where the crossbow was fired. It's only empty air right above the inner courtyard. On the second floor.'

'Yes.'

'Working on the hypothesis that the murderer had gone up to the roof and fired the crossbow while hanging from a rope, the police conducted a thorough investigation in search of signs of such an act, but they couldn't find anything. Don't you agree it's unbelievable?'

'That is really amazing. Is the murderer able to levitate? Or perhaps forces not of this world are at play.... Let's hear what an expert on the occult, actor and author of the best-selling *The Menacing Powers of the Spirit World*, Mr. Mitarō Anoyo, has to say.'

'It is clear, absolutely clear, that certain powers—what I'll call occult powers—are behind this. There is no denying it,' the middle-aged man declared forcefully, yet with a pensive expression.

'Oh, occult powers. Could you be more specific?'

'Let's say, for example, a kitchen knife or some blade was utilised in a murder. The strong feelings of grudge and resentment of the victim will seep into that weapon. The weapon itself carries the will of the victim who has passed to the other side. It will fly around, to enact vengeance on the murderer who killed them. I myself have been witness to this phenomenon twice.'

'Mr. Anoyo, you actually saw that with your own two eyes?'

'As true as I'm sitting here.'

'So coming back to our case, the crossbow flew around the house and murdered Ms. Mitsuko Kawamura. Does this mean that the person who murdered Mr. Kikuichirō Hachisuka was in fact Ms. Kawamura?'

'Yes, I'm sure of that. Karmic retribution, as they say.'

A crossbow flying around freely in the house? Kyōzō frowned at the suggestion.

Had that silly story of Tamiko's been leaked to the press? Or had Tamiko really seen a flying crossbow, and was this expert on the occult actually right?

Kyōzō shivered as a chill ran down his spine.

He was actually cold, of course. He wasn't afraid of ghosts.

The Midori woman apparently felt the same about the air. She bowed her head to the occult expert with a smile on her face as she switched to the next segment.

'Thank you very much. And now, the air has become quite dry of late. But I have good news for those young ladies among us who worry about their skin—.'

Kyōzō pondered for a while about the connection between skin care and the murder, but then noticed they had moved on to a commercial, so he switched the television off.

It had been utter nonsense of course, but he had a better idea of what was going on because of the programme. The arrow had hit Mitsuko at an almost level angle, which meant that the murderer couldn't have shot the crossbow from above the roof of the covered gallery, as Chief Inspector Tamura had proposed. It would also have been too far away. And, as it turned out, no traces had been found on the roof, so the method Kinoshita had fallen victim to was out as well.

But how had the murder been committed, then? If it had been impossible to do it from above, could it have been committed from below? Had the murderer used stilts? Would someone be able to use a crossbow under such unstable circumstances? And why would anyone commit the murder in such a manner anyway?

Had Ichio really solved the murder?

Kyōzō sighed, and decided he'd need to listen to what Ichio had to say.

CHAPTER SIX: ICHIO DENOUNCES THE CULPRIT

1

Three o'clock in the afternoon. Kyōzō arrived at the Hachisuka residence right on time, and several journalists who had been hanging around quickly ran up to his car.

'Inspector Hayami? Any comments on Mitsuko Kawamura's murder?'

'Has Yūsaku Yano been released? Do you truly think he's innocent?'

'Do you believe in the occult?'

'*Ein* comment, *bitte schön.*'

It was at this point that Ichio arrived, pushing her way through the crowd. 'Okay, okay, please make some room… Out of the way!' She was followed by Shinji, and together they climbed into Kyōzō's car.

'You actually came on time. I guess you realised you won't be able to solve this case without your dear little sister Ichio?'

'Hmm, I'll believe it when I see it. For now, I'm just keeping a promise.'

Kyōzō activated his car sirens and drove up to the front gate. He opened the window and pushed the button of the intercom.

'Are those two in the back also police officers? Miss, have you ever considered a career as a model?'

What a noisy bunch, Kyōzō thought. Are they really here to work on a news story?

He identified himself over the intercom and the gate opened. Needless to say, the journalists couldn't follow him inside.

Plainclothes police officers had fanned out all across the garden, combing the grounds for clues. The crossbow still hadn't been found, apparently.

'The two of you are supposed to be Yukie's friends, all right?'

His siblings nodded. Shinji was fairly calm, but Ichio was sparkling with excitement.

'Can't wait! Hehehehe. Today I'll be the star.' Ichio grinned in a creepy manner.

'I only hope you're right,' muttered Shinji under his breath.

'Oh, Shin is sooo jealous! Just because he didn't solve it himself.'

'I'm not jealous.'

'Yes, you are.'

'No, I am not.'

'You are sooo.'

As Kyōzō looked at the two, he realised it was probably too late for him to teach his siblings what "sanctity of life" meant.

Once inside the house, Kyōzō decided he would first meet with his colleagues from the S Police Station to get the details on anything that hadn't been clearly explained on television. Shinji and Ichio went directly to Yukie's room, supposedly to cheer her up as her friends.

Kyōzō found Chief Inspector Tamura, who had set up base in the parlour, and asked for updates.

'I'm sorry I'm late. I heard the case has been going in a strange direction.'

Tamura frowned at Kyōzō.

'…It certainly has. Can't make anything out of it.'

Tamura's explanation didn't differ much from what had been said on television. He did add that the distance from which the crossbow had been fired hadn't been precisely established, but it couldn't have been more than six metres, based on the force used.

'So it could even have been fired from very close in: for example, from within the room?'

'Yes, that's possible. But that doesn't seem likely, as nobody could have come in from the roof.'

That was true. Nobody could have entered Mitsuko's room without being seen by either Kyōzō or Kinoshita.

'I know it's a pretty silly idea… but have you considered stilts?'

Tamura waved his hand.

'I've considered that, too. Impossible. We didn't find any traces of stilts on the lawn in the inner courtyard. Trampolines, radio-controlled machines… we've considered all of those. We're still searching the house for anything out of the ordinary, but I'm not hopeful. And I don't think the murderer used any of those things either, myself. Why would he?'

Kyōzō saw the point Tamura was making. It was important to think the way the murderer would have thought.

'Have you heard that Tamiko said she saw the crossbow?' asked Kyōzō as he suddenly recalled that episode.

Tamura scowled as he nodded.

'Yes, I heard that one. But… well, you know….'

'But just for argument's sake, couldn't you attach the crossbow to a long rod, lift it up high and then fire it? Or perhaps hang the crossbow from the roof with a rope... Perhaps that's what Tamiko saw.' Kyōzō voiced all the possibilities that came to mind.

'Even supposing the killer could have done that, how would he have known the exact position of his target, Mitsuko? It would have been a miracle to even graze her, let alone make a clean hit through her heart.'

Tamura was right, of course.

'No, you're right, sir. Sorry, these ideas lead nowhere.'

'No, tell me any fancy ideas you might have. As things stand right now, I'll try anything,' sighed Tamura.

Yoshie Yano arrived at that moment with tea for the two detectives. However, after pouring it, she remained in the room. She looked as if she wanted to tell Kyōzō something.

'Is there anything the matter?' asked Kyōzō, which seemed to convince her to speak.

'Actually, it's just a small thing, but I remember something unusual. But er, I don't know of course whether it has anything to do with the case....'

Tamura leant towards her.

'Please tell us what you know, no matter how trivial it may seem,' he said softly.

Yoshie thought for a moment about how to phrase it, and then spoke hesitantly: 'It happened on the night of the first murder— the murder of Mr. Kikuichirō. Every night at midnight, either my husband or I go around the house to lock up the windows and doors and to dim the lights in the hallways. My husband wasn't here on the night of the murder, so I was the one to do the rounds. It was then that I noticed that the light in the covered gallery on the second floor had burnt out.'

'The light? Is that so unusual?' asked Tamura disappointedly.

'No, that's not what I meant. When I say light, I don't mean any of the fluorescent lights, but the small light beside them, the nightlight. We always keep that on during the night. There was nothing wrong with the fluorescent light, but the bulb of the nightlight seemed to have burnt out. I thought I could swap it for a new one the following day, so I didn't touch it. But then that murder happened, and I forgot all about the nightlight until today. Now I remember that night, when there was all that commotion and we went up to the gallery, the nightlight hadn't burnt out after all.'

Diagram 4

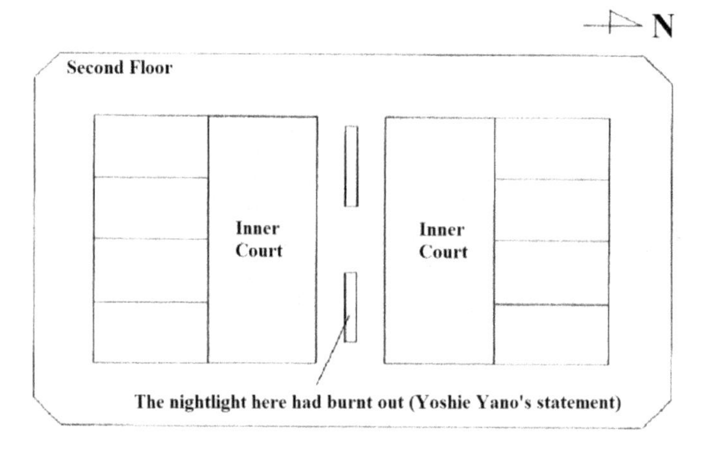
N
Second Floor
Inner Court
Inner Court
The nightlight here had burnt out (Yoshie Yano's statement)

‘It hadn’t burnt out? Are you sure? Couldn’t you have remembered it wrongly? Perhaps it wasn’t the nightlight on the second, but the first floor?’ asked Kyōzō, discouraged because it didn’t seem as though it had anything to do with the case.

‘I’m not mistaken. The nightlight in the covered gallery on the second floor had definitely burnt out the first time I was there. Somebody must’ve swapped the bulb between midnight and three o’clock. I can even prove it: one of the spare bulbs is missing.’

‘Does everybody in the house know where you keep the spares?’ asked Tamura, who had become rather more interested now.

‘Yes. They’re in the storage, and anyone can get in.’

‘Well, then, somebody noticed the lamp had burnt out and was nice enough to put a new bulb in.’

‘Not likely! My husband even has to swap the bulbs in their own bedrooms for them. They would never dream of touching any of the the lights in the hallways, let alone a nightlight! It was also only one of several nightlights, so it wasn’t as if the gallery had become pitch-dark. That’s why I didn’t think it necessary to replace it right away.’

‘Whereabouts in the gallery is this light?’

‘On the east side. On the other side from where Mr. Kikuichirō was lying.’ (See diagram 4)

‘…So that would be where the murder was actually committed.’

Tamura put a hand to his chin and thought for a while, then turned to Kyōzō: ‘Hayami, I think we’ll have to take a look at this. I think there are two possibilities.’

‘And what would they be, sir?’

‘The first possibility is that the murderer of Kikuichirō swapped the bulbs for some reason. Though I can’t begin to imagine what that might be at the moment. The other possibility is that someone else happened to have swapped the bulb, and in that case—.’

‘—It’s possible they might have seen something.’

‘Precisely. Anyway, working out who swapped the bulbs might become a valuable clue as well. Let’s check it out right away.’

Just at that moment, a uniformed police officer entered the room.

‘Chief Inspector! Yukie Hachisuka and her friends are demanding to be shown Mitsuko’s room. What should I do?’

Kyōzō clicked his tongue. Another of Ichio’s antics.

‘I—I’ll take care of that, sir.’

‘All right.’

Tamura turned back to the police officer and gave orders to look into what had happened with the nightlight.

As soon as Kyōzō left the parlour, he hastened toward Mitsuko's room. As he had feared, Ichio was having it out with the officer on guard there. Shinji and Yukie were standing beside her, unable to control Ichio.

'I told you, I'm here to help with the investigation. You're a slow one, aren't you? Oh, big bro, here, here!'

Expressions of relief appeared on Shinji and Yukie's faces as they saw Kyōzō coming.

Kyōzō slowed down in order to maintain his air of authority and spoke to the officer, while avoiding any eye ontact with Ichio:

'Ahem. What's the matter, officer?'

'Sir, these people want to take a look inside this room.... Is she your sister, Inspector?' asked the young police officer, his face flushed.

'Ye—No, I don't know her. Never seen her in my life.' Kyōzō felt so embarrassed he prevaricated. '...But I don't suppose they can do any harm. Crime scene investigation is already finished, and I'll stand watch, so they can have a quick look. You remain here and watch the hallway.'

'You watch the hallway,' repeated Ichio with obvious amusement.

'Shaddup, Ichi—Miss. Listen, you aren't to touch anything inside. Got it?'

'Yeeeees.' Ichio cheerfully raised her hand in the air.

'All right. You, open the door.'

The door was opened to reveal a dark bloodstain at about the same height as Kyōzō's solar plexus, and a small but deep hole in the door. There was also a white string in the outline of a human attached to the door, like a practice target. Had this figure been here before? Kyōzō asked himself. The large amount of blood which had seeped into the target hadn't completely dried out yet, and the dark, black stain created an obstacle at the entrance.

Yukie turned pale and put her hand to her mouth. Was she reliving the horrible scene? She ran off in the direction of her own room.

'Miss Yukie! Are you all right?!'

She turned around at Kyōzō's call and nodded. That was a relief to Kyōzō.

'Hehehehe, so that's it.'

Ichio was talking to herself as she handled the doorknob.

'Hey, don't touch that!'

'Does it really matter? You already checked it for fingerprints, didn't you?'

'That's true... but you shouldn't touch it anyway!'

Shinji, meanwhile, was touching the hallway wall, apparently in search of something. He observed that there was a tear in the wallpaper at the spot where the knob would hit the wall when the door was opened.

'What are you doing?' asked Kyōzō.

'Hm? Oh, I have my own ideas about the case, so….'

Ichio heard that and wasn't about to let it slide.

'What? So you think my deduction is wrong?'

'You haven't even told me what your deduction is, so how am I supposed to know whether you're right or wrong?'

Ichio stuck her tongue out and smiled.

'You're right, of course.'

Leaving the police officer outside, the three Hayami siblings entered the room.

'Is everything as it was this morning?' asked Shinji, looking around.

'Yes,' replied Kyōzō. Shinji, nodding vaguely, went over to the window and looked down.

'And the crossbow Tamiko said she saw was floating in front of the window right below this one, is that right?'

'Yes… But you don't believe that story, do you?'

Shinji, however, was lost in thought and didn't hear him.

'She said she saw the crossbow clearly because of the lightning, correct?'

'Yep. But, Shinji, I—.'

Shinji shook his head and stepped back from the window.

'It's unbelievable. The probability of this happening is….'

Did Shinji believe that what Tamiko claimed to have seen had really happened? What did he mean by probability? Had there been a series of coincidences, leading to an unbelievable event? Coincidence… did he mean the lightning?

Kyōzō gave up trying to follow his brother's line of thought.

'It's a pretty chic room. Oh, a nice sewing machine too. I'd love to have one of my own….'

'Ichio, you don't even know how to use it,' said Shinji coldly.

'Bah. Even I can—.'

'Do you really know how to use a sewing machine?'

'…No. But I still want one,' confessed Ichio honestly.

'Why did the two of you come here anyway?' exclaimed Kyōzō in exasperation, and Ichio quickly put her hand to her chin, pretending to be thinking hard.

'I see, I see, so the window was open.... Oh, I wish I had a full-length mirror as large as this one, too!'

Once again a spark appeared in Ichio's eyes. Kyōzō didn't even bother to comment. Anything he said would have an opposite effect, he realised.

'All these books are on dresses and accessories. ...Oh, look, here's a different book, *Teaching the Disabled*. What kind of person was this Mitsuko?'

'...She's the one who taught Yukie sign language. Don't know much else about her though.'

Both Shinji and Ichio were content with their quick look through the room.

'I'd like to see some of the other rooms as well.'

'Now hold it. First you'd better tell me about that deduction of yours.'

'Nooooo way. It's not complete yet. If you won't let me see the other rooms I definitely won't tell you.'

Kyōzō was about to yell at her, but bit his tongue.

'Who's next door?' asked Shinji as he pointed his thumb at the wall.

'That's Saeki's—Kikuichirō's secretary's room. But there's nothing I can do about it if he refuses to let you see it.' Kyōzō made sure his siblings understood that.

In fact, his warning turned out to be unnecessary, as Saeki welcomed them warmly, under the mistaken impression they, too, were police officers.

'Mr. Saeki, where were you last night?' asked Shinji politely, but with authority. He was trying to make it seem he was indeed with the police.

'In the study on the first floor working with the president,' came the immediate answer. Saeki had probably answered the same question countless times by now. He was neatly dressed and clean-shaven as usual, but his blood-shot eyes betrayed the fact he had not slept the previous night.

'At one o'clock in the morning?'

'Yes. The vice-president left behind an enormous number of documents that needed checking. The president said he needed help and we both knew it would be a late night for us.'

'Does something like that happen often?'

'Not at all, this was actually the very first time. When the vice-president was alive, work always proceeded very smoothly.'

'I see. That means you were very lucky then.'

'Eh? What do you mean?' Saeki looked puzzled.

'You see, if you'd been in your room last night as you normally are, you'd have been the first to be suspected, given your proximity to the victim,' explained Shinji suggestively.

'Oh, really? I hadn't even thought about that,' replied Saeki with a blank expression.

'What did you do when you heard Ms. Mitsuko scream?'

'Well, naturally I wondered what had happened, so I rushed out of the study. Then I heard Mrs. Tamiko cry out. I hesitated for a while about what I should do, when Mrs. Tamiko came out of her bedroom. She was very agitated, so I helped her first, and then went to talk to the Inspector.'

By the time Saeki had finished, Shinji had apparently already lost all interest in him, and was looking at the bookcase.

'You study quite a lot. Law, economics, politics. Is this the usual reading material for a secretary?'

'...I wouldn't know about that, but capable and efficient secretaries need to have great understanding of a wide range of topics, so I try to keep up.'

Kyōzō hadn't noticed it on his first visit, but the bookcase actually had double bookshelves—one front, one back—which meant it held double the amount of books he had initially estimated.

Shinji stuck his finger out and pointed towards one particular book. Kyōzō couldn't quite make out the title.

'Did you purchase that book recently?'

'...No, I bought it quite a few years ago.'

'Oh.'

Kyōzō assumed that Shinji's question had some ulterior motive, so he went over to the bookcase and peered at the book. It was *An Introduction to Typewriting in Japanese*. From the title and the condition, it was obviously quite old. Nobody would think of buying a book on typewriting now that word processors had taken over. Kyōzō cocked his head at the strange question his brother had posed.

Shinji appeared to have gone through all the things he wanted to ask. Ichio looked bored and yawned.

'We'll leave it at that.'

Kyōzō felt quite dissatisfied as he dragged his two siblings out of the room.

'And the room next door is the empty guest room where Kinoshita was staying, I assume? And next to that is Yūsaku's room. How did Kinoshita watch the hallway?'

'The door was open wide, so he could watch it from inside the room. He says he didn't take his eyes off the hallway even once.'

Shinji went over to the room and flung the door open so hard that the doorknob hit the wall.

'That wide?'

'Yep, that wide,' nodded Kyōzō. Shinji went in, sat down on the bed for a second and came out again.

'Looks as though it would be impossible for anyone to pass by in the hallway without being seen. I guess the only possibility is—.'

'Yep, that's the only way,' said Ichio, purposefully cutting him off.

'What? What are you two talking about!?' Kyōzō almost wept with frustration, but neither of them would give him an answer.

'Next stop, Yūsaku's room,' Shinji decided, and he knocked on the door.

2

'What were you doing up until the moment you heard the scream?' asked Shinji immediately.

'I was terribly tired, so I was already sound asleep in my bed at eleven,' replied Yūsaku.

He looked even more fatigued than Saeki and Yukie, perhaps due to his lengthy interrogation about the Kikuichirō murder.

'Yet you immediately jumped up when you heard the scream?'

'…I don't even remember whether I heard the scream or not. I woke up suddenly and noticed something was going on outside, and then I heard somebody yell downstairs.'

'Downstairs? That would be Mrs. Tamiko screaming, not Ms. Mitsuko.'

'I assume so. I have no clear memory of hearing Ms. Kawamura scream.'

'How much time passed between you hearing Mrs. Tamiko scream, and you getting out of your room?'

'Hmm… five seconds? Ten seconds? Something like that, I think,' said Yūsaku, without much confidence.

'You came out of your room about five or six seconds after I reached Mitsuko's door, so I'd say that's about right,' confirmed Kyōzō.

Shinji had no further questions.

Ichio had not been paying any attention to her brother, but was standing near the window with her arms crossed, looking out. From time to time she'd pretend to hold a crossbow and cock her head.

Shinji looked for a while at Yūsaku's bookcase, which was stuffed with study books for university. Then he seemed to remember something.

'Oh, I almost forgot something important. I think you said that Kikuichirō's body had been moved. I'd like to see that too.'

'Oh, that's easily done. Let's go.'

The three said goodbye to Yūsaku and headed for the connecting gallery.

'Look, you can still make out the bloodstains.' Kyōzō pointed to the black stain on the carpet. 'And the body was lying there.' (See diagram 1)

Shinji stared at the stain for a while and then took several measured paces.

'One, two, three. About three metres. So the body was dragged to the west side of the gallery for a mere three metres. It doesn't make any sense… No, wait. From the centre of the gallery, it's one step and a half to the east… and one step and a half to the west… The 8 Mansion… 8….'

Kyōzō suddenly recalled the testimony Yoshie had given earlier and looked up at the ceiling. It was still light outside, so the lights were naturally switched off. He looked for the switch and found a dial on the wall. He walked over to the wall, and turned the switch to ON. The fluorescent lights in the gallery all lit up.

'What are you doing?' asked Ichio curiously.

'Oh, it's nothing, something about a bulb being burnt out or not,' said Kyōzō as he turned the switch to NIGHTLIGHT. The lights went out and, while it was hard to see because of the brightness outside, he could indeed make out that the nightlights were on.

Kyōzō muttered to himself. There was nothing wrong with any of the lamps now. But what did that have to do with anything?

'Care to tell me about it?'

Egged on by Ichio, Kyōzō briefly explained what Yoshie had told him.

'According to her, this nightlight over here had burnt out when she checked at midnight on the night Kikuichirō was murdered. But the lamp worked when she was awakened at three o'clock and came here again. She's convinced that someone put in a new bulb between midnight and three. The Chief Inspector is working on that, I think.'

Shinji frowned, but didn't say anything, as he walked up and down the gallery.

'Perhaps she was just mistaken?' suggested Ichio.

'That's what I thought, but she said they were short one of the spare bulbs. I suppose she could have miscounted them, but—.'

Shinji suddenly stopped pacing up and down and asked: 'What did Yukie say about that? Was the nightlight on that night?'

'I don't know. I'll have to ask her later. But I don't think the two of them would have been able to see Kikuichirō in the gallery or the arrow in his chest if the nightlight had indeed burnt out.'

'So we can assume the lamp did work at one o'clock. That means the murderer changed the bulb before the murder occurred. But why?'

'What? Shinji, you can't just decide it was the murderer who swapped the bulbs.'

Shinji paid no attention to Kyōzō's protests, and walked off again.

'...Perhaps they couldn't have done it without the light... But they could have switched on the usual fluorescent lights... and the moon was bright enough for the witnesses to notice a figure inside a dark room—.' Shinji suddenly stopped and looked up.

'Shin, did you think of something?'

Shinji ignored his sister and looked across at Yukie and Yūsaku's rooms in turn.

'It's the 8... Because that nightlight had burnt out, it had stopped being a perfect 8.... That's it. The murderer wanted a perfect 8! That's why the nightlight had to work....'

'Shin...? Hello, Earth to Shin.'

Ichio was waving her hands in front of Shin's eyes, but Shinji brushed them away.

'Stop it, Ichio. I'm trying to look the part.'

'Ah, you're back. I beg your forgiveness, hahahaha.'

Shinji slowly turned to face the other two. He coughed once and said: 'O, Bacchus![xiii] Er, no, I mean, eureka[xiv]! That's what I wanted to say.'

Ichio opened her eyes wide in surprise.

'Eh? So do you have it now? You really know? The trick behind Kikuichirō's murder? No, wait, wait! Don't tell me just yet. I want to think about it myself too.'

'What are you saying!? This isn't some quiz programme! Shinji, have you really solved it?'

'Yeah. It's simple once you know the trick. The 8 Mansion. The peculiarity of the house. The fact the body was moved. The curious murder weapon: a crossbow. The role of Mitsuko Kawamura. And what clinches the deal: the nightlight. I'd have noticed it right away if only I had considered all these facts together earlier!'

'How was it done? Who did it!?' asked Kyōzō impatiently.

'That I still don't know. Anyone could have used the trick. It's not a clue to the identity of the murderer. Anyway, I don't think this is the time to tell you yet. I'll tell you once I know who the murderer is. There are still a lot of people I haven't met yet.'

3

Kyōzō had been put on hold for the solution to both the Kikuichirō and Mitsuko murders for the moment, so he was forced to continue dragging his two siblings around the house.

In Kikuji's room, Shinji took a look at the bookcase but only found a few books there between all the empty bottles, so he quickly lost interest. His eyes wandered to the film collection, which held well over two hundred titles.

'Oh, wow. You own almost all of Hitchcock's films!' he shouted excitedly. 'I see you like mystery films. There's *Murder on the Orient Express*. Do you like Christie?'

Kikuji blushed. 'No, I'm not a particularly big fan of mystery films, although I do like all of Hitchcock. My main interest is films starring Bergman.'

'Oh, I love her films, too. I knew you reminded me of someone. You're the spitting image of Gable,' said Shinji. Kikuji could hardly contain his joy as he tried to keep a straight face.

'What? You don't say! I don't look anything like him. Oh, but er, Shinji your name was, right? It seems we get along quite fine. How about a drink? I only have bourbon here, though.'

Kyōzō was reminded of Mori-no-Ishimatsu as he looked at Shinji[xv]. He acted out the perfect man from Edo.

'Shinji! Mr. Kikuji, we didn't come here to chat. Where were you last night?'

Kyōzō had decided to do his own work.

'I couldn't get to sleep last night. You understand, I'm sure? It's obvious that Yūsaku killed my brother, and now I had to sleep with him beneath the same roof. I was afraid something might happen. I knew the police were here as well, of course, so I hadn't expected another murder.'

He shook his head in disbelief.

‘So you were awake at the time Ms. Mitsuko screamed?’

‘Yes. I came straight out of my room when I heard it. You know what happened next. But, Inspector, why won’t you arrest him before he commits another murder?’

‘You mean Yūsaku?’

‘Who else!?’

‘No matter who we arrest, we need evidence. Also, at the very least, Yūsaku is innocent of the murder this morning. I understand your feelings, but in a case of murder we have to act very carefully.’

‘Oh, I never knew the police investigated cases carefully. You learn something new every day,’ said Kikuji sarcastically, and Kyōzō had to fight back his anger.

‘Shinji, Ichio, let’s go.’

They had finished everyone on the second floor and moved down to the first floor.

Kikuichirō’s widow Setsuko was holding her head in her hands, suffering from a hangover. As far as Kyōzō knew, she only had three modes: dead drunk, asleep after getting dead drunk, or suffering from a hangover after waking up again.

‘What do you want?’ she asked irritably, her fingers placed on her temples.

‘I’d like to ask you what you were doing last night around one o’clock,’ said Shinji. He was getting used to playing a police detective.

‘I told you I was sleeping. How often do I need to tell you? Owowow…’

Her raised voice was apparently echoing in her head.

‘When did you wake up?’

‘Half past one, I think.... Saeki was banging the door so loudly I had to get up.’

‘So you didn’t hear the scream? The others all woke up in surprise, you see.’

Setsuko scowled at Shinji.

‘What else do you want me to say? I was drunk, you know! Any problems with that?’

‘Oh, no, absolutely no problems. But it does mean you’re the only one who can’t account for her movements at the time of the murder.’

‘What do you mean account for my movements? I was here in this room. Where else would I be?’

‘The other people all took five minutes at most to meet with someone else after the murder. That’s not proof of their innocence, of course. But in your case, nobody saw you for thirty minutes. I imagine one could do quite a lot in thirty minutes.'

Kyōzō frowned at Shinji's thinly-veiled suggestion. Setsuko had the same reaction.

'And what exactly do you mean by "a lot"?' she asked in an uneasy tone.

'Something like this, for example: you're aware the murder weapon has disappeared, I'm sure. The police still haven't found it, even though, theoretically, nobody could have left the house after the murder. But you, in fact, would have had such an opportunity—.'

'If that's a joke, it's in very bad taste! I don't even remember what time I went to bed! Do you really think that, in such a state, I could have killed someone and gone out to hide the murder weapon?'

'It would have been very difficult if you were indeed drunk. But you might have been pretending....'

She glared hatefully at Shinji and shrieked: 'You can investigate all you want to see if I was drinking! I'll blow into your balloons and do all the other tests you have!'

'Oh, but testing now would be meaningless. You could have drunk something after the murder,' replied Shinji, smiling at her.

Setsuko blushed and her lips quivered, but she sighed in defeat.

'Very well. Arrest me if you want. See if I care.'

'Please don't misunderstand me. I'm not saying you are the murderer. But I don't deny the possibility either.'

Kyōzō decided that it would be dangerous to let Shinji play police detective any longer, so he quickly took the two outside. After they were some distance from the room Kyōzō said, in a low voice: 'Shinji, what game are you playing!? Do you think she's the murderer?'

'No, I only got caught up in the moment. I really hadn't intended to push her like that at first, but it was so much fun.'

Kyōzō and Ichio looked at each other, and shook their heads.

'Oh, it's quite rare to see three siblings together nowadays.'

They had properly introduced themselves this time, and Kikuo Hachisuka actually seemed quite pleased to see them.

'The younger two do look like each other, but you don't look anything like them at all, detective.'

'Yes, I take after our father. They always say these two look more like our mother,' explained Kyōzō, but Kikuo wasn't listening. He was staring straight at Ichio.

'You look just like Tamiko when she was young. She used to be the talk of the town back then. And even now she is, haha! It was only after what were effectively duels to the death with several other men that I managed to win her hand. Those were the days.'

Kyōzō hadn't been expecting much from Kikuo from the beginning, so when the old man started boasting about the old days, he lost interest.

Shinji, however, had something he wanted to ask, and he interrupted Kikuo in a loud voice: 'Sir, I think you were working here late last night, together with Mr. Saeki?'

The expression on Kikuo's face suddenly changed, and he shook his head vigorously.

'Saeki? No, I can't recall ever having duelled with anyone called Saeki before.'

'I'm not talking about a duel. Last night, when Mitsuko Kawamura was killed, you were here in this room working on some documents, is that right?'

'I thought it was Kikuichirō who got himself killed….'

Shinji was usually levelheadedness personified, but even he had to work hard to hide his annoyance.

'Kikuichirō has indeed been murdered, but it was Mitsuko Kawamura who was murdered last night. Please try to recall what happened.'

Suddenly Kikuo's face brightened, and he clapped his hands.

'Yes, that's right. I remember now.'

Kyōzō had his doubts about that and mumbled something to that effect. Kikuo suddenly cried out, as if to admonish Kyōzō. His ears at least were still working.

'Of course I remember. I'm not senile yet. Hachisuka Construction ca—.'

'Is it true you were here in the study around one o'clock, when Mitsuko Kawamura was murdered?'

Kikuo looked a bit offended because he hadn't been allowed to finish his slogan, but he answered nonetheless: 'Yes, that is so.'

'And the secretary, Mr. Saeki, was also here at the time?'

'Yes, we were here together. He was helping me work through the documents.'

'Were you together all the time? Do you remember the moment you heard the scream?'

'The scream? Whose scream?'

'Mitsuko Kawamura's scream of course!'

Shinji himself was on the verge of screaming as well.
'Don't know about that. I do know Tamiko was going on about something.'
Shinji frowned and thought about that answer.
'Hey, Shinji, you can see for yourself that this old man's not reliable.' Kyōzō whispered in Shinji's ear with his hand as a cover, to make sure Kikuo's sharp ears wouldn't pick it up.
'I believe it was you who designed this house?' Shinji ignored Kyōzō's warning and continued with his questions.
'Yes, that is so. Do you like it?'
'Yes… terribly… It's a terribly well-designed house. Never before in my whole life have I seen such a nice house,' replied Shinji suggestively, as he watched Kikuo's face. Kyōzō felt there was something important hiding behind Shinji's façade. The words his brother had uttered earlier came back to mind. He had talked about the peculiarity of The 8 Mansion. Was Shinji suspicious of Kikuo because it was he who had built the house?
But contrary to Kyōzō's expectations, Shinji's praise had Kikuo beaming, like a child who'd got full marks for a test.
'Yes, yes, you think so too? You might be young, but you have an eye for these things. What about it, would you like to work here? It just so happens we have an opening for the position of vice-president right now, so if you'd be happy with that….'
The three quickly made their way out of Kikuo's study.
'What gives, Shin? You can't really be suspecting that old man, surely?' Ichio apparently had the same impression as Kyōzō.
'No, I just wanted… you know, to see if I could bluff him into something.'
'So you do have your doubts about him!'
'But the way that man starts to dodder is abnormal. You'd think he'd do a more convincing job if he was only acting….'
'Is there such a thing as doddering in a convincing way? Anyway, that man is truly, really, genuinely going senile. I'd swear to it.'
'…I suppose so,' sighed Shinji.
'But you should've taken up that offer of the vice-president! You'd be settled for life then!'
'…Ichio, you're half-serious about that, aren't you?'
Shinji blinked in surprise.
'Ah, you knew?'
Ichio stuck her tongue out at him.

They went to see Tamiko, but they learned nothing more than what Kyōzō already knew, so they left quickly and visited the Yano couple's room on the ground floor.

'At midnight I checked whether everything was locked up, as usual. They said it might rain, so I made sure all the windows were closed. We were both asleep at half past twelve,' said Takao.

'What did you do after you heard the scream?' asked Shinji. Takao and Yoshie looked at each other and seemed embarrased.

'Actually, I didn't hear the scream at all. I sleep very soundly. It takes quite a lot of commotion to wake me up.'

'What about you, Mrs. Yano? Didn't you hear the scream either?'

'I'm sorry. I always wear earplugs to sleep. My husband snores horribly.'

Yoshie glared at her husband, and Takao's bearded face turned red.

'So you didn't hear anything until Kikuji called for you?'

'Er, that's right.'

Shinji thought for a while, and then proceeded to his next question.

'Mr. Takao, I take it you can handle a crossbow quite well?'

He posed the question nonchalantly, but it was enough to startle Takao.

'Yes... Although I'm not really skilled enough to boast about it. And lately I haven't had much time to go up into the mountains.'

'But you're probably at least as skilled, or even more so, than Yūsaku, I assume? And you, Mrs. Yoshie? Have you ever gone with your men to hunt?'

'No, I could never do it! My specialty is preparing the food!'

Her denial was quite vehement, but as Kyōzō looked at her large, strong arms, he thought that she might indeed be able to handle a crossbow.

'That was it! It's all over. And now the two of you will tell me what you know!'

Kyōzō shot a glare at his two siblings the moment they had left the Yano room.

'Nope!' Ichio cried.

'Why?'

A smile appeared on Ichio's face.

'You know why. The only proper way to solve a mystery is in front of all the suspects,' she said as she winked at Shinji.

'—She's right, you know,' agreed Shinji.

‘Have you any idea what you’re saying!? This isn’t some game! I’ve had enough of your—.’

Kyōzō became infuriated with them; he commanded them, he coaxed them and cajoled them, but they would not budge.

‘Let’s get everyone together. I think everyone will fit in the parlour here,’ Ichio ordered her brother loudly.

4

The three arrived at the parlour. It was already occupied by Chief Inspector Tamura, Detective-Sergeant Okuda and two police officers.

Kyōzō could feel the cold sweat on his skin as he explained the circumstances to Chief Inspector Tamura, who frowned as he weighed his options. Okuda was standing next to them.

‘You’ve got to be kidding! What can a bunch of amateurs tell us about this case!? In the first place, Inspector, I surely hope you have not forgotten that as a policeman, you have a duty to confidentiality? That applies to your family members as well!’

‘Bu—but the investigation has run into a stop now, so….’

Flustered, Kyōzō was attempting to find an excuse, when Shinji, standing behind his brother, spoke up calmly.

‘Have you found the crossbow?’

There was no answer.

Shinji grinned.

‘Haha, you still haven’t. So I can assume you haven’t searched there yet…,’ he mumbled, in a way that was audible to all present.

‘There? Where’s there?’ Okuda jumped on Shinji’s words.

‘Eh? Oh, no, I was only talking to myself. I mean, there’s absolutely no way the police wouldn’t have considered a place which even an amateur like me would think of, is there?’

His statement was followed by silence. Kyōzō, who had a good idea of what Shinji was trying to do, kept his mouth shut.

A nerve in Okuda’s forehead twitched violently, but he finally managed to speak with what was, for him, a very calm tone: ‘O—of course. But, er… suppose we listen to your suggestion anyway? What have you found?’

‘Oh, but are you going to listen to what a mere amateur has to say?’

An ugly scowl appeared on Okuda’s face.

‘Well, even the police occasionally have to lend a humble ear to suggestions from the public….’

'And if I did just happen to find the crossbow, would that imply you should lend an even humbler ear to an amateur like me?'

'Tha—that's....'

Okuda looked in the direction of Chief Inspector Tamura in search of help.

Tamura looked at Shinji with interest, and said: 'You seem confident. Are you perhaps in possession of some knowledge we don't possess?'

'No, absolutely not. All I know is what I heard from my brother. All I did was combine all the various facts, which told me one place the crossbow might be. I'm not completely sure it will be there, and you may even have already searched the place.'

'...Hmm. And where might that be?'

'If the crossbow turns out to be there, would you give me permission to assemble all the residents and solve the mystery in front of them?'

Tamura reflected for a moment and then nodded decisively.

'Very well, I agree. Well then, where's the place?'

'Hachi's kennel. The kennel in the inner courtyard. Over there.'

Everyone, including Ichio and Kyōzō, looked in the direction Shinji was indicating.

'The kennel? But I thought the inner courtyard had been searched extensively... Hey, you!'

Okuda called for a young police officer, probably in his twenties.

'Yes, sir?'

'Check the place out!'

'But I already searched there,' said the police officer, with a bewildered expression.

'You did? Hahaha! See, we already searched the kennel! There's nothing there. Too bad for you, you won't be able to do your little mystery solving show,' jeered Okuda triumphantly.

Shinji, however, showed no signs of disappointment and addressed the police officer: 'Did you dig in the ground?'

'Eh? Where?'

'Inside the kennel, of course!'

'No, I didn't go that far. You see, that dog is so large, and sometimes gets so ferocious....'

His voice became feebler and feebler until it became inaudible.

'...Shall I, um, take another look?' he asked, in a pitiful whine. Chief Inspector Tamura and all present nodded unanimously.

With quite some effort, two police officers managed to lure Hachi away from the kennel. After digging for a few minutes inside, they retrieved a lot of junk, and also the crossbow.

And, of course, Kinoshita's organiser was also there.

It was precisely five o'clock in the afternoon. The nine inhabitants of the house—Kikuo, Tamiko, Kikuji, Setsuko, Yukie, all three Yanos, and the secretary Kazuo Saeki—together with Kyōzō, Shinji, Ichio, Chief Inspector Tamura, Detective-Sergeant Okuda and several uniformed police officers, were all assembled in the parlour, packed like sardines in a can.

'What's this all about? Yoshie, could you pour one out for me?' asked Setsuko of Yoshie Yano. Was it the hair of the dog, or was Setsuko getting an early start on her evening drinking?

Yukie and Yūsaku were sitting right next to each other with anxious expressions on their faces, while Kikuji looked as if it all had nothing to do with him. Tamiko glared eerily at her surroundings. Kikuo was nodding in a carefree manner, as if a dinner party were about to start. Saeki's face was expressionless, but he couldn't hide the fact that he was anxious. There was no place for the Yano couple to sit down, so they took their positions standing next to the cupboard.

Shinji whispered in Tamura's ear:

'Chief Inspector, what did you find out about that nightlight?'

'Nothing. All of them claimed they knew nothing about it. I had the light bulb checked just in case, but there were no fingerprints on it,' Tamura whispered back.

Suddenly Ichio jumped up and started talking as if she were about to make a speech.

'Ladies and gentleman, we are gathered here today for one purpose: to expose the culprit behind the murder of Mr. Kikuichirō several days ago, and of Ms. Mitsuko Kawamura last night.'

'You are, young miss? Oh, this does sound interesting.'

Kikuji appeared to be genuinely fascinated by it all and leant forward eagerly.

'To be honest, there are still a few things I haven't worked out yet, but Shin here will cover for me on those points. So, let's begin!'

Ichio continued in a more relaxed manner.

'I shall start with the murder of Mitsuko Kawamura last night. I assume you're all aware of the circumstances, but I'll briefly recap the facts. Last night, my brother—Inspector Hayami over there—and his subordinate Kinoshita were staying here in the house. Kinoshita was watching the north hallway from inside his room, while Inspector Hayami was patrolling up and down the west hallway. Soon after one o'clock in the morning, someone screamed, and the inspector hastened to Mitsuko's room. By the time he arrived, Kinoshita had already made his way out into the hallway as well, closely followed by Yūsaku, coming out of his own room. Yukie and Kikuji came running from the south wing. Am I correct?'

Kyōzō, Yūsaku, Yukie and Kikuji all nodded simultaneously.

'By the time the door had been unlocked and opened, it was already too late! Mitsuko Kawamura had been cruelly murdered and there was no sign of the murderer inside the room. All the paths leading to the room had been under the surveillance of Inspector Hayami and Kinoshita. Because the window in the room was open, they considered the possibility the murderer had entered and left through there, but subsequent investigation showed that to have been impossible. The television coverage speculated that the killing had been the work of supernatural powers, but was this really a crime impossible for any human being to have committed?'

Ichio stopped and looked around. Nobody answered her question, so she had to do it herself.

'No, it was not. One person—actually two persons, to be precise, but let's say one person for now—one person had the opportunity to kill Mitsuko Kawamura.'

Everybody in the room started looking at each other, in search of the murderer.

Ichio looked slowly at everyone in the room, then finally continued: 'This person however is sadly enough not here in this room at the moment. For that person is, yes, Inspector Hayami's subordinate, Kinoshita. Kinoshita is the murderer of Mitsuko Kawamura.'

5

Silence reigned for a moment, but then both Kyōzō and Chief Inspector Tamura simultaneously started to bark at Ichio.

'Impossible!' 'That can't be!'

Ichio, however, continued unflinchingly: 'Kinoshita conjured up some excuse to enter Mitsuko's room without the knowledge of the inspector. After he murdered Mitsuko, he closed the door behind him and swiftly returned to his own room. That's all there was to it.'

'But what could his motive possibly have been?!' exclaimed Kyōzō, trembling furiously. Ichio shrugged.

'…I don't know. That's for you to find out.'

'Where had he hidden the crossbow all that time?'

'Who knows? My guess would be the empty guest room. You probably overlooked the loft above the bathroom or something like that.'

Detective-Sergeant Okuda coughed loudly.

'All the rooms, whether they were empty or not, were thoroughly examined. There was no crossbow anywhere!'

'Then Kinoshita brought it in with him secretly.'

'Secretly? That gigantic crossbow? Of all the people here I know best he wasn't carrying anything like that with him when we entered this house!' shouted Kyōzō, almost apoplectic.

'Then the crossbow was probably hidden by Mitsuko. My reasoning is as follows: Kinoshita and Mitsuko Kawamura were accomplices in the Kikuichirō murder. Due to the fact the doors and windows of the house had been sealed, creating an apparent locked room mystery, the possibility that someone from outside the house could be involved was completely overlooked. But as long as there was an accomplice inside the house, someone from the outside could have committed the murder. I don't know how it was done yet, but the two worked together and framed Yūsaku for the murder. And then Mitsuko probably tried to blackmail Kinoshita last night. Taking care that Inspector Hayami wouldn't notice him, Kinoshita sneaked into Mitsuko's room and murdered her. Mitsuko screamed as she was attacked, so Kinoshita ducked out of her room and back to the empty guest room. What Inspector Hayami saw wasn't Kinoshita coming out of his room, it was Kinoshita going back into his room.'

The more Kyōzō listened to Ichio, the more he started to think she might actually be right. At any rate, it was more probable than occult powers from the other side. And it all appeared to add up.

Shinji, however, let out a loud sigh, and signalled to Ichio to take a seat.

'My apologies, everyone… Ichio had been acting giddily about having solved the mystery earlier, so I already had my doubts, but even I couldn't have imagined she'd come up with something as ludicrous as that. I apologise to you all on behalf of my sister.'

'Shin, you think my reasoning is wrong?' pouted Ichio, her cheeks puffed up like a chipmunk.

'Of course. It's preposterous.'

'But there was nobody else who could have done it. I suppose our brother could theoretically have pulled off the trick equally well. But he wouldn't—.'

'You should know better than to have your emotions interfere with your logic. If you're determined to suspect Kinoshita, you should equally well suspect our brother.'

'Shinji, are you saying you think I—?' asked Kyōzō in disbelief, but Shinji waved him away.

'Not at all. I knew from the start that the murderer had to be one of the inhabitants of this house.'

'But who did it then? If both big bro and Kinoshita's testimonies are true, nobody could have committed the murder!'

'Precisely. Shinji, if there was a way, please tell us.'

Chief Inspector Tamura, too, was leaning forward.

Shinji returned each and every gaze fixed on him. Kyōzō was about to explode when Shinji finally began to speak.

'I was troubled for a while by Mitsuko's death. Not because of how it was done. It was absolutely clear how it was done. What troubled me was the reason why the murderer had utilised that particular method. But I eventually concluded that the murderer simply hadn't had the time to devise a meticulously planned murder for Mitsuko, as he'd done for Kikuichirō. The killer had only been saved by coincidence. That's in all probability what happened.'

'Can you stop with all the hints and cryptic allusions? It's getting on my nerves,' growled Kyōzō.

'Getting on your nerves? Oh, that's unfortunate. I'm afraid I'll be getting even more on your nerves, then.'

'Even more on my nerves? What do you mean?'

Shinji shot a meaningful smile at Ichio and announced: 'I will now lecture on impossible crimes.'

CHAPTER SEVEN: SHINJI DELIVERS A LOCKED ROOM LECTURE

1

'Lecture? What are you talking about?' bellowed Kyōzō angrily.

'The American mystery novelist—some say he was British because he lived there for a long time—John Dickson Carr wrote a novel called *The Hollow Man*[xvi]. In it, Dr. Fell says the following: "I will now lecture on the general mechanics and development of the situation which is known in detective fiction as the 'hermetically sealed chamber.' Harrumph. All those opposing can skip this chapter." This is followed by the *Locked Room Lecture*, which is said to have been the inspiration for Edogawa Rampo's essay *A Classification of Tricks*[xvii].'

As Shinji paused for a moment, Kyōzō managed to get a word in.

'And you plan to give a locked room lecture as well? You must be kidding.'

Okuda and Tamura nodded their heads vigourously in agreement.

Nevertheless, Shinji continued doggedly.

'I intend to hold this lecture because it is intricately connected to my investigation of the Kikuichirō and Mitsuko murders. So please bear with me.

'Now, due to the particular characteristics of this case, the terms "hermetically sealed room" and "locked room" are not strictly accurate. Setting the Kikuichirō murder aside, you remember the window in Mitsuko's room was in fact open. So what I intend to do is to deliver a lecture on locked rooms in the broad sense of the term—what Rampo calls "quasi-locked rooms."

'First of all, I obviously need to define what I mean by a quasi-locked room. Strictly speaking, what we call a locked room is a room which is perfectly sealed. Entering or leaving the room is utterly impossible—of course, that's only the surface appearance. On the other hand, there are also situations where there is a space which might not be physically sealed, but which—due to circumstances such as the testimony of eyewitnesses or footsteps left on the snow—is deemed to have been impossible to enter or leave. That's what I'm calling a quasi-locked room.

'As you know, the doors in this house all have push-button locks, which means that a key is necessary to unlock them from the outside, but not to lock them after a crime has been committed. I hope this clarification shows that, in neither case, are we dealing with actual locked rooms.'

'So that makes these cases easy to solve?' snorted Okuda.

'...I didn't say that. I am merely defining the terms. Allow me to continue.

'In both our cases, there are other elements which make them different from a classic locked room murder. Normally, in detective fiction, such a murder usually means there's a corpse inside a room, but it appears impossible for the murderer to have entered or exited, or to have hidden anywhere in the room.

'In the Kikuichirō murder, however, it wasn't the location of the body which created a locked room situation, but the location where the murderer was thought to have been. In the Mitsuko murder, the only reason it became seemingly impossible was because of where the murderer was thought to have been when the crossbow arrow was shot. The killer didn't need to enter the room itself, but it would have been impossible for him to have shot the crossbow while hovering several metres above the inner courtyard; nor could he have fired the weapon from the covered gallery, *et cetera*.'

His audience had stopped protesting and was now listening attentively. Satisfied, Shinji continued his lecture.

'With all of the foregoing in mind, I will begin my analysis.

'Let's start with one of the most common classifications of the quasi-locked room: the room not physically locked but under observation. This classification is relevant to one of our cases.

'What I mean is that, due to both Inspector Hayami and Kinoshita being on guard, nobody could have entered Mitsuko's room. Possible categories:

1. One witness is lying (or both are). Ichio has already talked about this, so I assume there's no need for further explanation. The theory that either Kinoshita or Inspector Hayami himself could have committed the murder falls into this category. There is also the possibility, of course, that they themselves are not the murderer, but are lying in order to protect someone else.

'The next category is rather crude when used in fiction, but very possible in real life:

2. The murderer passed by without being noticed by either of the witnesses. In the case of the second murder, it seems well nigh impossible for anyone to have gone undetected by Inspector Hayami, but what about Kinoshita? He was watching the hallway from inside the room, from his bed. It's quite possible he could have missed someone sneaking past the open door of his room. But it seems highly unlikely Kinoshita would have missed someone returning from Mitsuko's room after her scream had put him and everyone else on high alert.

'So, now on to the next category, which is very suggestive:

3. The murderer was in the victim's room long before the crime was committed. In the case of Mitsuko's murder, that would mean they were already inside her room when she and Inspector Hayami went downstairs together.'

'But then the murderer would have no way to flee the scene! Or are you suggesting they jumped out of the window!? Everyone in the house would have heard that,' protested Kyōzō after some reflection.

'Wait a minute. I never claimed that this possibility was what actually happened. One can also divide category 3 into two sub-categories:

3a. The murderer had entered the room long before the crime, and after the murder, either managed to escape without being seen, or remained hidden inside. The second part overlaps with category 2.

'The second sub-category is:

3b. The murderer had entered the room long before the crime, but committed the crime and fled the room at a time earlier than the assumed time of the murder. In other words, the scream Inspector Hayami and the others in the house heard was in fact not Mitsuko's.'

'But that was definitely a woman screaming, and I'm sure it came from her room,' objected Kyōzō as he drew on his memory of events.

'In passing, I should mention that detective novels often use a gunshot as the sound used to determine the time of murder. The murderer uses a silencer or a pillow to muffle the sound of the actual shot then, at the time they want witnesses to think the murder happened, they reproduce the gunshot sound using a tape recording or somesuch. But this explanation, of course, doesn't apply to the Mitsuko murder. That's because we know she was still alive at the time Inspector Hayami and Kinoshita started their surveillance, and even if the murderer had killed her right after that, they still wouldn't have had any chance to escape unseen.

'So now we arrive at the final category of the room under observation:

4. The murderer committed the crime from a location outside the field of observation of the witnesses, and fled. It's this explanation that applies to our case, as no other explanation fits.'

Shinji made his declaration with much self-confidence. The other people in the room looked in bewilderment at each other. They were wondering whether there was some deeper meaning behind what Shinji had said.

'What's the point of telling us that now? Nobody saw the murderer, so of course that's what happened! We know they shot the crossbow from above the inner courtyard. The question is how they managed to fly up in the air,' sneered Okuda at Shinji's absurd theatricals.

'I'm eliminating all the possibilities one by one. I understand it's a tedious process, but bear with me,' replied Shinji.

'A human being is not able to float several metres in the air without the help of some form of mechanical assistance, and the police investigation has shown that no such device was present anywhere in the house, so we can consider Mitsuko Kawamura's room, including the space above the inner courtyard outside her window, as one large sealed space, or locked room.

'I shall now present a rough classification of the types of locked room—including the quasi-locked room. Rampo classified three types, but I divide them up in four categories.

'Somebody thought to have been murdered is found inside a room that nobody could have entered or exited, or at least, such appears to be the case. How could it have happened?

'The first explanation is that the murderer did enter the room, committed the murder there and left. They could have played with the time, as in the example I mentioned just now, or they could have tampered with the lock in a way that nobody noticed. However, we've already eliminated this possibility in relation to the Mitsuko murder.

'The second explanation is that, while the death appears to be murder, it actually is not. For example, we should at least consider the possibility that Mitsuko committed suicide using the kind of trick used in Conan Doyle's *The Problem of Thor Bridge*[xviii].'

'Suicide? Who in the world would commit suicide with a crossbow? Nonsense!'

It was Okuda who once again sneered at Shinji's lecture and Kyōzō had to agree with him.

'He's right, Shinji. Also, Mitsuko wouldn't have screamed like that if she'd committed suicide, and also the crossbow would necessarily have to have been left in the room.'

Listening to his brother made Shinji sigh.

'Didn't I just tell you, it's *The Problem of Thor Bridge*! Don't you even know your Sherlock Holmes? That's incredible... Anyway, leaving out the details, Mitsuko could have used some kind of trick to make the murder weapon disappear after she died. But such a mechanism would have had to have left traces, both in the room and on the crossbow. So I have to agree with you here. Eh, you needn't look so surprised. I'm simply examining each and every possibility.

'And now for the third explanation. The murderer did enter the room and did commit the murder there, but didn't leave the room. Which means that the murderer is still hiding in the room, or perhaps has burnt their own body until there's nothing left but their bones,' said Shinji, smiling broadly.

'Wha—what did you say?' exclaimed Kyōzō.

'What I mean is that if there had been a big incinerator in the room, the culprit could have committed suicide after the murder. But, of course, you made sure that there was nobody inside Mitsuko's room, dead or alive, didn't you?'

'Of course! There was nobody except for Mitsuko in that room, no cut-up body or ashes or anything else!'

Kyōzō's hair was starting to hurt. The eyes of those who had initially listened seriously to Shinji were beginning to glaze over.

'Thank you for your hard work. Finally, we come to the fourth explanation: the culprit committed the murder without entering the room. This can also be divided in two sub-categories:

4a. The victim was killed inside the locked room with the help of a device controlled remotely, or a device with a timing mechanism. But since, as far as I know, there are no remote-controlled flying crossbows, I think we may rule this possibility out.

4b. The victim was outside the room, and the culprit committed the murder outside. Then, either the culprit used some method to move the dead body back into the room, or the mortally wounded victim made his way back into the room unaided and died there.

'If you give the matter your full consideration you will quickly realise there are no other logical explanations for the locked room murder than those four.'

'Now what? You say those are the only four? But which of them is it?' yelled Kyōzō in frustration. 'You said the first and second were out, didn't you? And so was the third. So was it the fourth—the body itself was moved inside the room? And if so, how?'

'I never said that. What I said that Mitsuko Kawamura had to have been outside her room. But it would, needless to say, have been impossible to have carried Mitsuko's body back into her room and nail her to the door without being seen by the two police detectives on guard. And obviously, she didn't walk back into the room and nail heself to the door after having her heart pierced.'

'So what did happen, then!? If the murderer didn't do it, and she herself didn't do it, how did her body get into the room? I hope you're not going to tell me it was a natural phenomenon.' There was anger in Kyōzō's voice.

'A natural phenomenon? You could put it that way. It's definitely a matter of physics. I find it curious that nobody has thought about the possibility, even though it's been clear from the start that Mitsuko was killed by a projectile. It all becomes clear the moment you consider why Mitsuko was nailed to the door—.'

'Was there a reason for her to be nailed to the door?'

'A reason… as I said earlier, I believe it was all a matter of coincidence. But not in the sense you all seem to be thinking. For example, I don't mean to suggest that Mitsuko happened to spot the culprit, tried to run and ended up nailed to the door. For if that had been the case, she would have been shot in the back, not the front. Ask yourselves: why would she be standing by the door? If she wasn't trying to flee, why was she there?'

Shinji looked around the parlour room, but nobody offered an answer.

'Mitsuko had just stepped out of her room. But, as I said, not to flee from the culprit. She stepped out, and it was at that very moment she was shot from the front by the killer.'

'I don't understand any of what you're trying to say. Where was the murderer?'

'You still don't understand? The culprit was... standing next to Kinoshita's room, right in front of Yūsaku's room!'

2

Chief Inspector Tamura and Ichio cried out at the same time. They'd realised what Shinji was trying to tell them. Yukie couldn't cry of course, but she too was visibly shocked, her eyes opened wide and her hands covering her mouth.

Kyōzō, however, still didn't see the whole picture.

'But why did she get nailed to the door like that if the killer shot the crossbow from there? Are you trying to say the arrow flew in a curve?'

'It seems there are still people here who don't get it, despite all my explanations, so I'll explain it in chronological order. The murderer had probably been contacted by Mitsuko Kawamura and decided that she had to be silenced. He told her over the phone to step out of her room, and waited for her in front of Yūsaku's room, holding the crossbow. If he'd gone further down the hallway, he'd have been spotted by Kinoshita, of course. Mitsuko could not have imagined that she was about to be killed, given that there were two detectives in the house, so she was naturally not especially on her guard. The killer took aim from his position and fired at Mitsuko....

'The arrow pierced Mitsuko through the heart and pinned her to the door. The force of the impact caused the door to crash back violently against the hallway wall, rebound at high speed and slam shut, all in the blink of an eye! The miracle was only possible because Mitsuko was so small, and because the crossbow was so powerful. I doubt even the killer could have predicted it would happen.'

'Furthermore, as Mitsuko was leaving her room, she had pushed in the button of the lock in the doorknob, as she usually did, which is why the door became locked after it slammed shut. And that's why she appeared to have been shot through the open window.' (See diagram 5)

Everyone—even the doubtful Okuda—now grasped what had happened.

Diagram 5

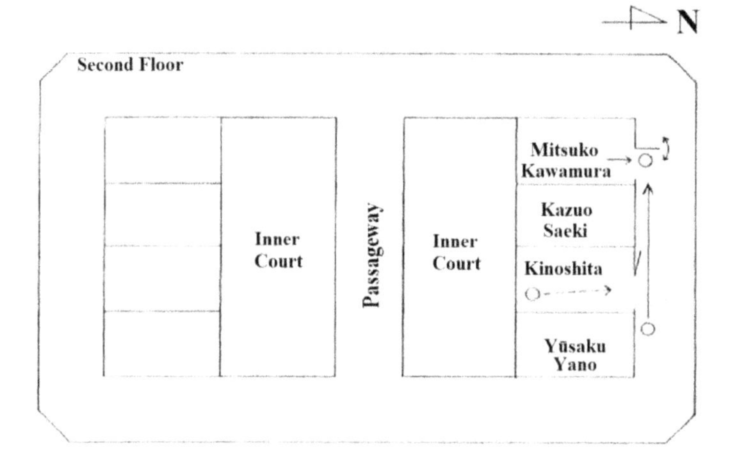
N
Second Floor
Inner Court
Passageway
Inner Court
Mitsuko Kawamura
Kazuo Saeki
Kinoshita
Yūsaku Yano

Kyōzō could clearly see the scene in his mind's eye... Mitsuko screaming out as she was nailed to the door. The door that banged against the wall and then flew back.

'I can't believe it....' Chief Inspector Tamura frowned.

'Oh, yes, when Mitsuko went out of her room earlier that night, she did indeed lock her room,' confirmed Kyōzō.

'When we visited her room, I examined the spot on the wall outside, where the doorknob had struck it,' explained Shinji. 'This house doesn't have any—what do you call them?—doorstops, so the doorknob hit the wall with full force, causing a fresh tear in the wallpaper in the process.

'The killer then fled the scene so as to avoid detection by the approaching Inspector Hayami, but quickly realised the situation had turned out to his advantage. If he now threw the crossbow down into the inner courtyard, the police would assume it had been fired from a spot above, because of the angle of the arrow. Or perhaps he tried to throw it inside Mitsuko's room, but failed.

'It was at that moment that Tamiko, awakened by the scream, looked out of her window. It was pure chance that lightning struck just at that moment, which made the crossbow appear to be suspended in the air. It also happened that the crossbow was facing her. It was really all a confounding series of coincidences. Almost as if John Dickson Carr's ghost himself had been behind it all.'

Shinji had intended the remark as a joke, but nobody laughed.

Kyōzō was impressed. So what Tamiko had seen had been neither an illusion nor a ghost!

He no longer had any doubts about Shinji's explanation. Yūsaku and the others looked with awe at him, as if he were some kind of star.

'But if things happened as you say, Shinji, why was the crossbow buried inside the kennel? Do you have any idea?' asked Chief Inspector Tamura, perplexed.

'Oh, that? That was the handiwork of Hachi, of course, who seems to have the nasty habit of taking whatever falls in the inner courtyard for his own. He dragged the fallen crossbow into his kennel and buried it along with his other treasures. When I heard about Tamiko's story, I immediately realised that the crossbow must have dropped somewhere below her room. But, if so, the police should have discovered the weapon right away. So why wasn't the crossbow there? The killer would hardly have dropped it there on purpose, only to hide it again somewhere else, so I concluded that a third party must have hidden it. And the only candidate was the dog,' explained Shinji, as if it were nothing special.

'So then who is the murderer?' asked Kyōzō, and the whole group held their breath as they awaited Shinji's reply.

But Shinji just shook his head.

'It's not important at the moment. I'm still in the middle of my lecture. There's still another locked room to solve.' And with that, Kyōzō's question was dismissed out of hand.

3

'And so we now return to the first murder. What we have here is a locked room situation in which the door is locked, and no secret passages or anything of the kind exist. The police have naturally also examined whether entrance via the roof or the room next door was possible.'

'Surely you haven't forgotten that Yūsaku was inside that room?' interrupted Okuda irritably, but his words lacked energy.

'Of course I haven't forgotten. The reason you think Yūsaku committed the murder is simply because you can't see how anyone else could have done it. So let's examine that and say, for the sake of argument, that Yūsaku was not the murderer. If, in the end, we conclude that it was indeed impossible for anyone else to have done it, then, by default, Yūsaku is the murderer.'

Okuda looked pleased with that. 'Ha, as if anyone else could have done it,' he snorted.

Yūsaku, who had been listening to the discussion, was obviously shaken.

'To continue,' said Shinji, 'Kikuichirō's murder, as I already said, is not a classic locked room mystery, so the categorisation I described previously doesn't apply. Let's go back to Dr. Fell's locked room lecture for a moment.

'The good doctor gives seven categories of creating a locked room murder when no murderer was in the room, apart from tampering with the key. They are: (1) a death appears to be a murder but in fact is not. (2) The murderer does not commit the murder themselves directly, but puts the victim in a situation where they kill themselves or die in an accident. These two possibilities fall under the second category to the locked room I mentioned previously, but don't apply in this case. (3) A mechanical device is utilised to commit the murder. Unless there's a remote-controlled crossbow out there somewhere, I believe we can ignore this one. Dr. Fell's fourth category is (4) suicide made to look like murder. I mentioned this when I discussed Mitsuko's murder. There were witnesses to Kikuichirō's murder, so this one doesn't apply either. Next up is (5), and this is a very special case. What happens here is that the murderer dresses up as the victim, so as to make it appear they are still alive. This case doesn't apply either, because there were witnesses to the victim's death, but one thing we do need to think about is whether the figure that Yukie and Mitsuko Kawamura saw in Yūsaku's room was really the murderer.'

'What do you mean "whether the figure was really the murderer"? If they weren't, who was?' Kyōzō was getting more confused by the minute. What was Shinji trying to suggest?

'I'm talking about the possibility that the figure the two witnesses saw wasn't the actual murderer, and that the real killer shot Kikuichirō from a different spot. I doubt the witnesses actually saw the arrow as it flew through the air, so it's a possibility.'

'The figure wasn't the murderer? So who was it, then?'

'Considering nobody else could have entered that room, my guess would be Yūsaku himself.'

Everyone's eyes turned to Yūsaku, who looked startled.

'I don't know what you mean… I was asleep.'

'That's right. You claim you were sound asleep. Let's assume you're telling the truth. That still doesn't mean you couldn't have been the figure in the window.'

Ichio looked up suddenly and stared intensely at Shinji.

'No way… you can't be serious, Shin… You're not trying to suggest anything as stupid as… No! You're saying Yūsaku suffers from sleepwalking?'

'Yes, but don't get me wrong, I'm only suggesting it as a possible theory. Yūsaku walking in his sleep—or perhaps just wandering around half-asleep—and opening his window, just at the very moment the murderer shot Kikuichirō from a different spot, out of Yukie and Mitsuko's line of vision, is a possibility we do need to consider.'

Although Kyōzō did think it sounded rather silly, he still needed to think about it.

'But that's quite a stretch, don't you think? You yourself said this was a premeditated murder. Nobody would plan a murder that depends on such a coincidence.'

'You're right, of course. Some of those present might not be aware of all the details, so let me explain. Kikuichirō's murder was a meticulously planned and diabolical crime. It used Mitsuko

Kawamura as an accomplice to make a witness out of Yukie, in order to frame Yūsaku. The culprit could not have foreseen in their plans that Yūsaku would stand near the window of his room in his sleep. Unless, of course, Yūsaku was accustomed to standing in front of his window at one o'clock every night in his sleep. So I feel we can rule out category 5 as well.'

Shinji was becoming thirsty from his lengthy lecture.

'Mrs. Yoshie, could I have a glass of water? Yes, water will be just fine, thanks.'

Shinji downed the glass of cold water he'd been given and continued:

'Where was I? Ah, yes, category 6 of Dr. Fell's lecture covers the case of someone inside a locked room being killed by a person outside. However, that's not relevant to our case, for it wasn't the victim who was in the locked room, but the culprit.

'Category 7 is also very interesting, but also not related to our case. It concerns the victim being still alive at the time the murder was thought to have taken place. Again, it's a trick that plays with time. It's the opposite of the one I mentioned when I was discussing the Mitsuko murder. Let's look at some examples of the murder having taken place earlier than thought, and later than thought.

'Inspector Hayami is already aware of this, but if the murder had not occurred at one o'clock, but at a later time, another person would have been able to commit it as well. That person is Yūsaku's father, Takao Yano. But in order to manipulate the assumed time of the crime, it would also have been necessary for him to change the time on the clock in Yukie's room. It also seems unlikely he would frame his own son, so I believe this category can be eliminated as well.'

Shinji stopped for a moment and looked around at all the people in the room. Okuda was clearly bored, Kikuji looked very entertained, Yūsaku and Yukie appeared anxious, Kyōzō was obviously eager to know the truth as soon as possible, and Ichio was thinking very hard in the hopes of keeping up with him.

'And the eighth explanation?' prompted Chief Inspector Tamura, but Shinji shook his head.

'There isn't one. That's as far as Dr. Fell's locked room lecture goes.'

Okuda suddenly brightened.

'Ha! So that means that in the end, only Yūsaku could have done it. I knew it! I knew it would turn out like that—.'

'Are you hard of hearing? I said that was it for Dr. Fell's locked room lecture. But the dear doctor himself says the following: "It's only a rough offhand outline, but I'll let it stand." Listen, when do you think *The Hollow Man* was written? In 1935! That's more than fifty years ago. Since then, many detective writers, including Carr himself, have searched for new variations on the locked room. As you might expect, very few truly outstanding variations have been invented since the so-called Golden Age passed. Most of them are simple rehashes of the variations covered in *The Hollow Man*. Some critics have even declared that no new types of locked room will ever be invented. But as of late, writers have been appearing in our own country who present us, not with rehashes, but completely newly invented tricks. For example—and I think some of you might have read it already—Jirō Akagawa comes up with a trick to murder someone inside a hermetically sealed room in *The Deduction of Tortoiseshell Cat Holmes*—a true locked room with no means in or out[xix]. And he didn't use a gun that would go off on its own after a while, or some automatic mechanism or anything like that. And then there's—.'

'Nobody cares about your books! Does this have anything to do with Kikuichirō's murder?' barked Kyōzō, who had just about had enough.

Shinji cocked his head, and apologised: 'Oh, I did get a bit carried away there. What I wanted to say was that there are still so many possibilities out there.

'Anyway, the reason I talked for so long about Carr was not simply because I wanted to refer to his locked room lecture. From the very beginning of this case, I felt his hand present. The way Yukie and Mitsuko Kawamura witnessed the crime made me think of one of his novels, entitled *The Emperor's Snuff-Box*, and that's what led me to the theory that Mitsuko was an accomplice to the murderer. And the murder weapon itself, a crossbow, invokes Carr's medievalism. Also, the crimes occurred inside a house shaped like number 8, which is what made me first suspect that the murderer might be a fan of mystery fiction, like myself. And that perhaps they were very familiar with Carr. Once I started thinking along those lines, I quickly managed to see through it all. What put me on the scent were Carr's *The Hollow Man*, and the work of another mystery novelist who was very friendly with Carr, whom I will now talk about.'

'So you're finally going to reveal the truth?' asked Kyōzō with a sigh of relief.

'It'll take just a little bit longer. Please be patient for a few more minutes.

'There were several authors of the Golden Age who were on very friendly terms with each other, and who would talk about detective fiction until the early hours. Carr and Ellery Queen for example. Carr's novel *The Curse of the Bronze Lamp*[xx] in fact came into being as a result of talks between the two of them—or maybe I should say the three of them, since Queen himself was a collaboration between two cousins. There was another writer who was good friends with them: Clayton Rawson, who's not very well known in Japan. The only one of his novels you can readily get your hands on here at the moment is *Death from a Top Hat*[xxi].

'Carr and Rawson sometimes wrote stories based on ideas—impossible situations—that the two of them had exchanged. The idea proposed by Rawson was that of a room disappearing completely, and Carr's short story *The Crime in Nobody's Room* was based on that. Carr's idea was that of a man disappearing from a telephone booth under observation, and the story Rawson wrote based on that idea was—.'

'*Off the Face of the Earth.*[xxii]' interjected Ichio.

'Yes, Ichio, have you read it?'

'Yes, but how do that story and *The Hollow Man* relate to this case?'

'Keep listening. The reason I mention *Off the Face of the Earth* is because it's a special case which doesn't fit within any of Dr. Fell's categories. But as I explained earlier, since this isn't a locked room murder, it's only natural that it wasn't covered by the lecture. Have you noticed the similarities between the story and our case? In *Off the Face of the Earth*, a man seen entering a telephone booth manages to disappear from there, despite two policemen watching the booth. In our case, we have two witnesses seeing a person inside a room he couldn't have entered. It's basically the converse situation.'

'And, how was it done in *Off the Face of the Earth*?' asked Kyōzō.

'…I don't really feel like revealing the trick to people who haven't read it. Well, very basically put, it's an optical illusion. Calling it just a simple, honest mistake of the witnesses might be going too far. It was, of course, the culprit's intent to mislead the witnesses. The manner in which they were fooled is, of course, of utmost importance, but I can't really say that Rawson succeeded….'

Shinji shook his head sadly.

‘Eh? What? So after that long, rambling commentary, you’re going to say that it boils down to Yukie making a mistake? That she didn’t see what she thought she saw?’ asked Kyōzō, stupefied.

‘Anything wrong with that?’

‘Of course! Nobody will accept that as an answer! Now Mitsuko Kawamura is dead, the whole explanation of Kikuichirō’s murder depends on Yukie’s testimony. What are we supposed to do if you say she made a simple mistake!?’

Shinji let out an amused sigh.

‘I see. I suppose you’re not going to believe me unless I let you see for yourselves. Just as The Great Merlini did.’

‘See for ourselves? What do you mean?’

‘What I mean is that I will reconstruct for you what the culprit did that night. Mr. Takao, do you have your keys with you? Oh, no, you can wait here. Yūsaku, do you have your own key? You don’t? Okay, please go up to your room and get it. Make sure to lock your window and door when you leave. Oh, and you there….’

Shinji addressed one of the police officers. It was the man who had dug up the crossbow.

‘Yes?’

‘You go up with Yūsaku and make sure everything is bolted.’

The two looked puzzled, but left the room as asked. Even Okuda was caught up in the moment and didn’t voice any protests.

‘The rest of you can go up to Yukie’s room. Actually, you might not all fit in there, so those not interested can remain here. Ichio, I’m casting you in the role of Kikuichirō, okay?’

Ichio nodded in disappointment. She hadn’t managed to solve the mystery herself in time.

‘Chief Inspector, could I perhaps borrow the crossbow? No? Well, that shouldn’t matter. It might not look as good without the murder weapon, but let’s raise the curtain on our murder play,’ said Shinji with a smile on his face.

CHAPTER EIGHT: KYŌZŌ TAKES UP SIGN LANGUAGE

1

All the occupants of the house, plus Kyōzō, Okuda and Tamura tried to gather in Yukie's room, but they could not all fit and several of them had to wait outside. Shinji's "murder play" had to be viewed in turns.

'Your brother is the centre of attention,' observed Okuda to Kyōzō in amusement. But then he muttered to himself: 'Stupid games....'

'Okuda, you shouldn't talk like that,' said Chief Inspector Tamura, admonishing him. 'The ideas of amateurs occasionally remind us, the professional investigators, of things we might overlook because it's all become routine work for us. Besides that, what Shinji just explained does sound quite reasonable.'

'Sir! What I meant was that locked room murders and suchlike only exist in stories! People who commit murders in the real world do so because they are blinded by greed or driven to despair. They don't go around thinking about how to create a locked room mystery. At best they might have a friend lie for them in order to provide an alibi. In fiction, the most likely person is never the murderer. But in real life, they almost aways are!'

'I understand the point you're making. And you'd be right ninety-nine percent of the time. But this case might be the exception. As long as there's a possibility that Yūsaku is innocent—however small it may be—it's our duty to investigate that. We don't want the press all over us for leading a prejudiced investigation or being too rough during the interrogation, do we?'

Just at that moment, Ichio announced:

'Big bro? You can open the curtains there now!'

Kyōzō had been standing by and quickly drew open the curtains.

The first thing that came into view to the people packed into Yukie's room was the figure of Ichio, who was standing in the gallery waving her hands.

Through the windows of the gallery they could also see Yūsaku's room, as Kyōzō himself had noted the other day. Although the room had been locked tight, the window was open and they could make out the figure of Shinji standing there. The lights in the room were off, so as to replicate the situation on the night of the murder.

'How did he get inside? How did he get in there?' muttered Kyōzō, dumbfounded, but nobody had an answer.

'It's a trick! It has to be some kind of trick!' cried Okuda.

Shinji leant out of the window and, making sure everybody could see him clearly, made a finger pistol with his index finger and pretended to shoot.

Ichio clutched her chest, as if in pain, and fell to the floor.

That's really in bad taste, Kyōzō thought as he frowned. He stole a glance at Yukie, who didn't look very well.

'Yūsaku, Mr. Takao, I take it you both have your keys with you?' asked Kyōzō, and both of them showed him the keys they were holding in their hands.

Kyōzō dashed out of Yukie's room in confusion.

Had Shinji somehow learned how to pick a lock? Or had he learned acrobatics somewhere? No, no, both the window and the door had been locked.

He ran along the west hallway, heading for Yūsaku's room.

As he went past the connecting gallery he looked to his right, where Ichio was supposed to be lying.

He stopped in his tracks.

'That's odd.'

It wasn't that Ichio wasn't lying there in the gallery. She was indeed lying there. Two of her were, in fact.

And there had also been a familiar-looking man wearing a suit standing there, looking his way. It hadn't been Shinji.

Who was it? He desperately wanted to know how the locked room trick had been worked, but this came first.

He stepped back to the opening of the gallery.

There was indeed a man there. A large man. The man was standing at the east end of the gallery, his head cocked as he looked at Kyōzō. Ichio was sitting on the carpet, grinning at Kyōzō. Right behind her sat a girl wearing the exact same clothes, with her back to Ichio.

He took a step forward and so did the other man.

'No way….,' was all he could say.

Kyōzō had finally realised what was happening. He stood fixed to the spot with his mouth open, staring at himself.

He pulled himself together, just as the curtains of a room in the north wing were suddenly pulled back.

Shinji was waving at them from Mitsuko Kawamura's room.

2

They all returned to the parlour once again.

'So? Do you all understand now?' asked Shinji. 'I'll draw a diagram and explain it once more. Does anyone have a large sheet of paper and a pen for me?'

He borrowed a notebook and pen from Tamura, and drew a simple floorplan of The 8 Mansion. To that he added several straight lines.

'The murderer placed the large full-length mirror from Mitsuko Kawamura's room precisely in the middle of the gallery, with the mirrored side facing west. And, to make sure the inside of Mitsuko's room wasn't directly visible from Yukie's room, the curtains were closed. With that, the stage was set. Oh, no, excuse me, there's something else. There was one little thing that was threatening to mess up the murderer's scheme. The nightlight. One of the nightlights on the south-east side of the connecting gallery on that floor had burnt out during the night. So naturally, the culprit was forced to change the bulb—.'

'Why naturally? I don't see it,' interjected Kyōzō.

'Because the perfect symmetry of the 8 would have been lost otherwise. They could have switched off the nightlight on the north-west side of the gallery too, but then it would have been too dark to see. If they'd switched the usual fluorescent lights on, then there'd be symmetry, but also the fear that someone would notice the mirror. So the murderer had to exchange the nightlight. Okay? Then I'll continue.

'The murderer had arranged with Kikuichirō to meet him in the gallery at one o'clock. Kikuichirō came up the west staircase, to the west side of the mirror. Yes, the west side. Contrary to the statements of Yukie and Mitsuko, he didn't come from the east side of the gallery. What they saw was nothing but a mirror image. Kikuichirō himself naturally wondered why there was a mirror there.'

'The killer might have called out to him then, or perhaps Kikuichirō noticed them and approached the window of the gallery, when… the rest you know.' (See diagram 6)

Shinji opened his arms wide at the end of his explanation.

'…Wait, Shinji. So you mean that Mitsuko Kawamura was indeed an accomplice?'

'Yes, of course. That story about being assaulted was a flat-out lie. After she left Yukie's room, she probably hid behind the door and waited there. And it was she who attacked Yukie when she came out

Diagram 6

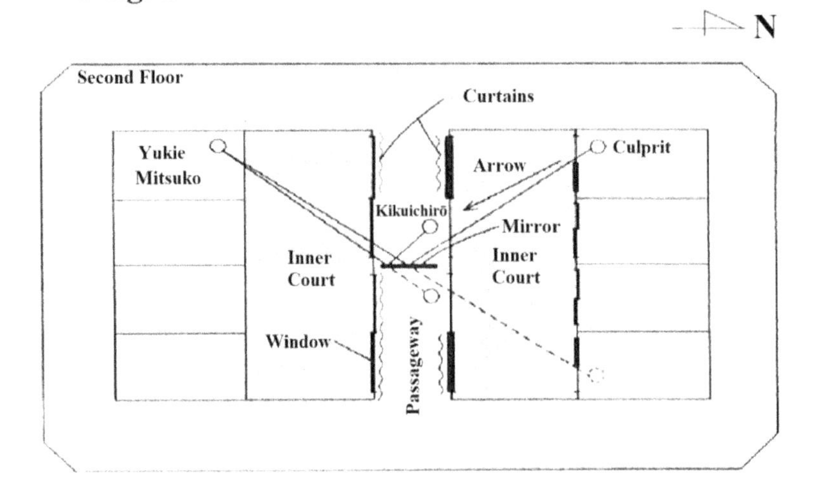
N
Second Floor
Curtains
Yukie
Mitsuko
Arrow
Culprit
Kikuichirō
Mirror
Inner
Court
Inner
Court
Window
Passageway

of the room worried about her. And I assume it was the culprit who knocked Mitsuko herself out later.'

'But why do all of that?' asked Chief Inspector Tamura.

'To give the murderer time to clear away the mirror and move the body, of course. The other people in the house couldn't be allowed to know a murder had been committed until all that had been done. That's an important aspect of this case. Now, why was the body moved? The police assumed that the murderer had tried to move the body in order to hide it, but had given up. But I think we can now work out the real reason. There was no point in trying to hide the body, given that there had been two witnesses to the crime. No, the culprit moved the body in order to obscure the real location where the murder had taken place. The body was moved from the west side, to the east side of the gallery.'

'Wa—wait. Wasn't the body found on the west side? You're not making any sense,' said Kyōzō, bewildered as usual.

'What I said is perfectly correct. The killer did move the body from west to east. But then they noticed that blood had been spilt on the carpet. Unless something was done to conceal that, the real crime scene would be obvious to anyone, and someone might think of the trick with the mirror. They must have been alarmed by the blood. But then he—or she—came up with a brilliant solution to the problem. They moved the body back to its original position. What remained was a body with obvious signs that it had been moved. But who would have guessed that the body had merely been moved back to its original spot!

'Right from the outset, I had a nagging feeling that things had turned out in the murderer's favour too often. Even though there were two witnesses, both had been knocked out, and the crime not reported until two hours later. And while it had been clear where the murderer had stood, there was no trace of him to be found at that spot. And why had the murderer only knocked the witnesses out, instead of killing them? To buy himself time, of course. But even the culprit and Mitsuko couldn't have guessed that the witness would be out for two hours. Five minutes would have been more than enough to return the mirror back to the room and move the body. Mitsuko must have hit Yukie much harder than necessary, I'm assuming.'

'I've a pretty good understanding now of what happened, Shinji. But if you're correct, who's the murderer?' asked Chief Inspector Tamura.

Shinji bit his lip as he reviewed his thoughts once more. It took a moment for him to continue.

'It's obvious that the first and second murder were committed by the same person. Despite an extensive search through the house by the police, they couldn't find the crossbow, which had been used in both murders. This means that unless there is another accomplice, we are looking for one and the same culprit for the two murders. We can discard the theory that there's another accomplice, though. If the killer had been able to count on the help of two accomplices, there would have been no need for such a convoluted plan.

'So if there's only one murderer, we can eliminate the people who couldn't have committed the first murder, and then the people who couldn't have committed the second, and then the killer must be amongst the group remaining. It will be a very small group by that time....'

'I see. So for the first murder, we can eliminate Yukie and Takao Yano, who has a clear alibi. For the second we can eliminate Yukie and Kikuji....' Kyōzō started to count on his fingers.

'That's right. And you and Kinoshita can be removed from the equation as well. And, according to Mr. Saeki's testimony, we can also eliminate Mr. Kikuo and Mrs. Tamiko for the second murder.'

'Yes, at the time of the scream, Mr. Kikuo, Mr. Saeki and Mrs. Tamiko were all on the first floor... But that means that the only person left is... Setsuko....'

Kyōzō suddenly froze.

'But Setsuko couldn't have done it. She's left-handed....'

'What's being left-handed got to do with it?' asked Chief Inspector Tamura in surprise.

'Sir, I forgot to report about this until now, but Yukie and Mitsuko Kawamura both stated that Kikuichirō's killer was left-handed. The only left-handed person in this house besides Yūsaku and Mitsuko is Setsuko, which is why I had my eye on her....'

'Ah, I see. But the witnesses had been in fact looking at a mirror image. So the murderer is right-handed. It's sloppy of you, forgetting about something as important as that,' added Tamura, but he did not appear very angry. Rather, he looked pleased they were heading towards the conclusion of the case.

'It is dangerous to assume that because someone is left-handed, they're not the murderer, but it does seem inconceivable someone would use their non-dominant hand on purpose, as it would draw suspicion. So we can leave Setsuko out.'

'I can't fault your reasoning, but where does it leave us? Who's the murderer? There's no one left.'

Shinji did not answer Ichio's question, but turned to the master of the house, Kikuo.

'Mr. Kikuo, do you remember the question I asked you earlier? About when Ms. Kawamura was killed? You told me you heard your wife screaming, but not Ms. Kawamura, is that correct?'

'Yes, I did say that,' said Kikuo confidently.

'... I think everyone here is aware that Mr. Kikuo's hearing is extremely sensitive. So how could he have heard Mrs. Tamiko's scream, but not Ms. Kawamura's scream some moments beforehand?' said Shinji. 'Here's what I think: Mr. Kikuo was not awake when Mitsuko Kawamura was killed. He was probably dozing off. And if that's true, the statement that Mr. Kikuo and Mr. Saeki had been together becomes questionable.'

He turned to face Saeki.

3

'Sorry, I don't really follow what you're saying,' replied Saeki calmly.

'Well then, even if I may be mistaken, please allow me to continue with my deductions. I hope you don't mind if I assume that you're the murderer, just for argument's sake? You knew the two police detectives had gone to Mitsuko Kawamura's room to grill her, and it made you anxious. Furthermore, those same two detectives were planning to stay the night in order to watch her. What if she succumbed to pressure and gave the whole game away? You became very uneasy, and decided to recover the crossbow which you had kept hidden somewhere. My guess would be that you had buried it somewhere in a corner of the garden. You offered to help Mr. Kikuo with the documents in order to create an alibi for yourself.

'You called Mitsuko and asked to see her, which would mean her leaving her room. Armed with the crossbow, you made your way quickly up to the second floor. The instant Mitsuko stepped out of her room, you shot her. She must have cried out when she saw you aiming the crossbow at her. That's when things started to go wrong for you. If she'd died silently, you'd have been able to sneak back down to the first floor to Mr. Kikuo's study and wait for Inspector Hayami to discover the body. You would only have needed to go up after the inspector had found the body and started a commotion.

'But you also had a lucky break. The door had been closed. You went down to the first floor, to the connecting gallery there. You opened a window and attempted to throw the crossbow up into Mitsuko's room from there, but either the crossbow was too heavy, or the distance too great. You missed and the crossbow fell down into the courtyard. That's what startled Mrs. Tamiko and caused her to call out. You hurried to her room and calmed her as she was coming out. From that point on, you had a solid alibi.'

A tranquil atmosphere spread throughout the room. Everyone was relieved that Saeki was the murderer.

4

'Okay, we've heard enough. Mr. Saeki, I must ask you to accompany me to the police station as a material witness,' said Okuda.

'I repeat what I said before. I'm not the murderer,' said Saeki, but Okuda didn't reply and placed his hand on Saeki's shoulder.

'When I went up to your room earlier, I became convinced you were the murderer,' said Shinji, with a faraway look in his eye. '*An Introduction to Typewriting in Japanese*! It didn't belong there. You told me it was a book you'd bought some years earlier, which was obvious. We all use computers and word processors nowadays. Nobody would buy a book like that for their studies today.'

'But what has that to do with anything, Shinji?' asked Kyōzō, once again confused. 'What kind of a connection could there be between that book and the murders?'

'The bookcase in his room consisted of two shelves, one in front and one in the back, and both were completely full. The older books, and books he didn't read anymore were in the back shelf of course, while newer books or books he often read were on the front shelf. But there it was, *An Introduction to Typewriting in Japanese*! And the other books around it were also old. That meant that he'd purposely moved the books that were usually in the back shelf to the front, and vice-versa. In other words, he had books he didn't want us to see.'

'Books he didn't want us to see? What, like *Sabu*[xxiii]?' Needless to say, it was Ichio who asked the question, which could have been serious or a joke.

Shinji was taken aback by his sister's comment for a second, but regained his composure and continued.

'I'm willing to bet that, on the back shelf, we'll find *The Hollow Man* and other works by Carr!'

'No! You're wrong! I hardly even read detective stories, and I certainly don't have any books by that Carr of yours.'
'Why did you move the books, then?'
'I just happened to have placed the books like that when I first moved in here, and I never got around to rearranging them anymore.'
Shinji looked dubiously at Saeki, but then an expression of surprise appeared on his face.
'Really? Do you really mean I'm wrong? That's a problem! If it's true, my whole case falls apart....'
To Kyōzō it didn't appear to be an important issue at all, but Shinji was visibly troubled by the revelation.
'Who cares about what books he reads or doesn't read? Anyway—.'
'Be quiet! ...Give me time to think. ...That's it! Could someone go up and check Mr. Saeki's bookcase? To see if there's a detective novel there.'
Even though there would have been no need for him to follow Shinji's orders, one of the police officers left the room hastily and returned after a few minutes.
'There are no detective novels up there,' he announced.
Shinji closed his eyes and fell silent.
The others didn't quite know what to do, so they sat looking at Shinji without saying a word.
Nothing happened for several minutes, but then a large smile spread across his face.
'In the masterpiece *The Nine Mile Walk*[xxiv], Professor Nicholas Welt says the following: "a chain of inferences could be logical and still not be true." To be honest, I wasn't seriously suspecting Mr. Saeki.'
In his mind, Kyōzō called Shinji a liar. He'd been more than serious about accusing Saeki.
'I can't deny that a lot of questions would have been answered if Mr. Saeki had indeed been the murderer. But I knew there were a few hard-to-believe points. I'm hardly in the position to say this about other people, but Mr. Saeki appears far from having the body strength needed to pull the heavy string of a crossbow. And then there's the matter of the timing. Inspector Hayami said he was in front of Mitsuko's door only seconds after she screamed. Ten seconds would be generous. And right after that, lightning struck and Mrs. Tamiko witnesses the floating crossbow.
'Could Mr. Saeki have gone down from the second to the first floor, opened the window of the connecting gallery—I already checked with Takao Yano that the windows were shut—and thrown the crossbow

out within ten seconds? Impossible, of course. Yet, because he seemed to be the only person left, I was sorely tempted to accept that theory. But it appears I was mistaken.'

A smile of self-deprecation appeared on Shinji's face.

'You were wrong? You mean, this guy isn't the murderer?' shouted Okuda, pointing at Saeki with a trembling finger. 'Then who is it!?'

'We eliminated the suspects one by one, which left us with Mr. Saeki. But he isn't the culprit either. In fact, there is one more suspect left. But the moment I solved the trick with the mirror, I fell into the culprit's trap and lost sight of him. Yes, I'm talking about you of course,' said Shinji, looking straight at Yūsaku.

5

Everyone was in disbelief.

'Impossible!' 'I—it can't be!'

Kyōzō and Okuda had cried out simultaneously and their voices overlapped, so their cries came out as: 'Impossicantbe!'

'Even as I speak, I can hardly believe it myself. However this time I'm finally confident I've arrived at the truth. Oh, his plan was incredibly elaborate. He deliberately planned to be accused of the first murder, only to be cleared of the crime later. The concept isn't new on its own, of course. As you all know, if you have ever faced trial, you can't be tried for the same crime a second time. There are also detective stories about people using that same concept to escape the hand of justice. That's basically what Yūsaku wanted to accomplish, too. But to think he'd corner himself into an impossible situation… is truly astonishing.'

Shinji was visibly impressed and nodded his head several times.

As for Yūsaku, a grin had appeared on his face, but his eyes had a glassy look and he did not appear at all like his usual self. Yukie, who was sitting next to him, had turned pale and was shaking her head slowly as she looked at him.

Yūsaku suddenly realised everyone's eyes were upon him. As he slowly looked around at all those assembled, he started to clap his hands in the direction of Shinji. Startled, Yukie moved away from him.

'Bravo! Bravo! You're amazing! I was afraid no one would work it out. But it seems there's a happy ending after all.'

While the words he uttered were highly peculiar, they did appear to be an admission that Shinji's reasoning was correct.

‘Yū—Yūsaku? What in heaven’s name did you do?’ Yoshie Yano called out in fear.

‘Shinji is completely right, mother. I created this,’ said Yūsaku triumphantly.

‘This? What?’ asked Kyōzō, in a daze.

‘All of it! The whole business! I had a bit of luck of course, and it was Shinji here who added the finishing touches, but… I am the creative mastermind behind it all.’ And, with that, Yūsaku started to snigger.

Kyōzō felt a chill run down his spine.

He had believed in Yūsaku all that time. Had this bright young man, seemingly framed for a crime he didn’t commit, in truth been an insane murderer all the time?

The others, too, had the same reaction, and looked at Yūsaku with surprise and disgust.

Shinji was the only person who appeared friendlier than before.

‘Yūsaku, there are a few things I’d like to confirm with you. What I understand the least is the Mitsuko murder. Why did you undertake something as perilous as that? I assume that, after shooting her, you ran back into your room to throw the crossbow away through your window, am I right? But that can’t have been part of your original plan. It’s just too sloppy. What exactly happened?’ Shinji was shooting questions at Yūsaku.

‘Oh, that? Things wouldn’t have turned out that way if she hadn’t tried to threaten me. I admit things got a bit messy, but what I was trying to do was to direct suspicion towards Mr. Saeki.’

‘Mr. Saeki? But there must have been better ways—.’

‘No. You see, I didn’t know. I’d been in my room all the time, so I wasn’t aware that he’d gone downstairs to work. I thought he was still in his room….’

If Saeki had been in his room, then suspicion would indeed have fallen on him, as the only person within the area under observation by Kyōzō and Kinoshita.

‘Shinji! Shinji! Could you slow down a little! I’m having trouble keeping up. Do you mean to say that the murderer—the person who killed Kikuichirō and Mitsuko—is really Yūsaku?’

Tamura seemed as if he was about to have a panic attack.

‘Precisely. He even confessed to it,’ replied Shinji, as if the question was trivial.

‘But… but the trick with the mirror: why do it at all?’

Tamura's point was valid. If Yūsaku was the murderer, he didn't really need to have used a mirror, or an accomplice in the person of Mitsuko.

'That was a trick Yūsaku *wanted* us to see through, because if no one did, it was he who would actually be convicted of the murder. I should have worked it out the moment I laid my eyes on the floorplan, but it took me until the very last moment to get there. There was an abundance of clues, from the moved body to the burnt-out nightlight, and still nobody managed to solve it! Yūsaku must havebeen getting really nervous. Of course, he could have pretended to solve the trick himself, if he'd really been left with no other choice, but that could have resulted in an opposite effect, making him appear more suspicious, in fact.'

'That's exactly right! When I dreamed up the plan, I thought the trick was so simple that even a child could solve it,' agreed Yūsaku cheerfully. 'But nobody managed to work it out. I was really getting concerned about what to do next.'

Kyōzō felt awkward and stared at the floor. It was embarrassing that a police detective couldn't work out a trick that any child supposedly could.

'So did you really do all of that, then?' asked Tamura, who still had not recovered from the shock.

'Yes, I actually performed that magic trick. I was careful to leave all kinds of small clues for you, but nobody saw through it. How could I have known that a police investigation would be so… unmethodical.'

'Bu—but you're left-handed! If you used the mirror trick, you must have shot the crossbow with your right hand!' protested Okuda.

Yūsaku looked scornfully at him.

'Of course I used the crossbow with my right hand! Right-handed people might use their right hand exclusively, but many left-handed people are somewhat ambidextrous, using their left hand for some actions, and their right for others. Didn't you know that?'

'So you planned for us to solve the mirror trick, and when we did so, suspicion would be deflected away from you if you used your right hand.'

The fellow was obviously as mad as a hatter —that was Kyōzō's conclusion, now that he'd regained his composure.

'The motive… what was your motive?' he barked.

Yūsaku eyed Kyōzō with surprise, but then he spoke seriously.

'My motive? My motive… at first it was Yukie. I don't know how Yukie feels about me, but one day, I realised I had fallen in love with her. Some time back, about two months ago, I half-jokingly asked Kikuichirō if I could marry her once I started working. I couldn't believe how enraged he became. It was at that moment I began to think that perhaps I should kill him.'

Yūsaku spoke as if in a dream. He didn't even notice Yukie getting up from the sofa and staggering out of the room.

'But then I came up with the brilliant idea of using the mirror to put myself in a desperate situation and then have my name cleared... It was as if I was looking at mathematical perfection. I was emotionally moved. From that moment, I even stopped caring about my original motive....'

To Kyōzō, this was further proof that Yūsaku was insane. No rational person would be emotionally moved by a murder plan.

'If I'd had a talent for writing,' continued Yūsaku, 'it might have just ended with me writing a detective story. Maybe that would have been preferable. What do you think, Shinji?'

'I suspect Kikuichirō and Mitsuko Kawamura would have liked that better.'

'Oh, that's right, Mitsuko! Why did she help you with such a deranged plan? Was she your lover?' asked Kyōzō as he suddenly remembered Mitsuko's role.

'No! I've already told you I'm in love with Yukie. Mitsuko Kawamura hated Kikuichirō, don't you see? I don't know the details, but it seems they were having an affair for a while.... It's the usual story of love going sour. I was only able to conceive the plan because I knew about them. If not for her, I couldn't have used the mirror, nor could I have had Yukie act as a second witness to the crime. Mitsuko and I simply happened to want the same man dead. No, it was inevitable. It was fate. I had to do it. It had all been arranged for me....'

'And killing her was also inevitable?' Kyōzō couldn't stand much more of this.

'Yes... I was sorry for her, you know. I hadn't wanted to kill in such a horrible manner. It was a sloppy plan, too. I was going to force her to write a note clearing me of the murder, and then kill her, making it appear like suicide. She has a lot of sleeping medicine, so it would all have appeared natural. But, as things turned out, it was a great success anyway. And I was even honoured by the unexpected appearance of a great detective....'

Yūsaku gazed admiringly at Shinji.

'It was wonderful... It was all truly wonderful.'

Yūsaku kept mumbling to himself until Tamura came to his senses and ordered Okuda to put him in handcuffs.

6

Several days later, on an afternoon at Sunny Side Up.

Kyōzō was dressed in the tailcoat of his much-respected grandfather, who like himself, had been a well-built practitioner of judo. It was as neatly dressed as he would ever be. He was holding a bouquet of roses in his right hand and a small book in his left.

'What's with the suit? Going to mingle with high society at the Rokumeikan[xxv]?' asked Ichio in surprise. It was the first time she had ever seen her brother like that.

'Is it too formal? I wanted—.'

'Wait, let me guess. Now the case has been solved, you're going to ask Yukie out for dinner. And the book there is about sign language.'

'How did you know?' asked Kyōzō, as he tried to hide the book.

Ichio put her index finger to her forehead.

'Making that mistake in the case has helped me polish my deductive skills. Don't you think so, Shin?' she asked of Shinji, who was pouring coffee for everyone.

'Eh? Yeah, sure,' he replied absentmindedly.

Just when the three siblings were finishing their coffee, Yukie entered the shop.

It was only after Kyōzō had jumped up and greeted her, that he noticed someone standing behind her.

It was Saeki.

'Oh, Mr. Saeki!'

Embarrassed, Kyōzō tried to hide his tailcoat.

'Yukie told me you'd invited everyone for dinner, and I thought this would be a good occasion to tell you the news.'

'The news?'

Saeki glanced at Yukie, who blushed.

'I've proposed to Yukie.'

Kyōzō's mouth dropped open.

Saeki had proposed to her? That puny-looking guy? But of course Yukie would never....

'And she gladly accepted. She was also in love with me, it seems.'

The world around Kyōzō was turning black. He couldn't see anything any more. He couldn't hear anything anymore.

Shinji noticed what was happening with Kyōzō and quickly took over.

'Oh, that's great to hear.'

'It is better to have something auspicious at a time like this, I thought. Yūsaku's confession was another reason for me to propose as well. And that's why the two of us would like to invite you for dinner tonight. It's all thanks to you.'

Kyōzō's lips were still quivering, unable to utter a single word.

'Dear brother, suppose we let these two lovebirds enjoy each other's company tonight? We can take them up on their kind invitation another time.'

Kyōzō nodded awkwardly.

'My brother agrees, so please have a nice evening together. No, no, you really don't have to thank us. Let's have dinner another time.'

After he had seen the two off, Shinji sighed loudly.

Nobody spoke for a while.

Outside the shop, the curtain of night had already come down.

Kyōzō had been standing motionless for almost twenty minutes, but eventually mumbled: 'Going home.'

Shinji and Ichio let out simultaneous sighs.

'Don't worry, there are still plenty of nice women out there. And you weren't really head-over-heels for her, were you? Not like that.'

'Of course. And you yourself are a good example, Ichio. You're cute, but still one of the leftovers.'

'Eh, is that supposed to be praise? I'm only twenty-one, you know? Plenty of time to get married.'

'True, but you don't have a boyfriend yet, do you?'

'What! That's just because I haven't had the good fortune to meet the right man yet….'

'That must be it. Anyway, I'm going home.'

Kyōzō thanked his siblings for cheering him up and headed for the door. He could feel the tears welling up, moved by his lost love, but also because of his siblings' support.

Ichio called out to her brother's back.

'You're forgetting something! Roses and your book!'

Kyōzō didn't turn around, but just shook his head.

'Throw them away,' he said woefully.

'You really don't want them? Okay, then they're mine. They're quite expensive!'

'Oh, that's on sign language? I was thinking of learning it myself. I'll take that.'

Kyōzō turned around to see his siblings cheerfully grabbing their spoils.

His lips quivered slightly.

'He—hey, you guys—.'

Kyōzō hadn't noticed the ringing of the cowbell behind him. A woman pushed the door open with her back. Her hands were holding a wheelchair.

'Hey, everybody! I see you're all here. I was released from the hospital today.'

The cheerful voice of Kinoshita was completely out-of-place. Both of his arms and both of his legs were covered in plaster.

Kyōzō hadn't noticed any of that behind his back, and was about to run out of the shop.

'Inspector, congratulations with solv—.'

Kyōzō was not directly at fault.

All he did was bump into Kinoshita's girlfriend.

She—Sanae Ogawa—cried out as she lost her balance, fell against the wheelchair she was pushing and let go of it.

The wheelchair with Kinoshita on it slowly rolled away from the shop.

'No—wait, Sanae! Stop me! Stop me now!'

As Kinoshita's arms were both in plaster, he couldn't put the brake on himself.

Kyōzō still hadn't fully grasped what was going on, and Sanae was still lying on the floor near the entrance.

Outside the shop, the road slanted slightly to the right. Kinoshita's wheelchair slowly turned right and started going down the slope. Three female high school students going back home from school saw the scene, but cruelly did nothing but laugh.

'No, Kinoshitaaaaa!'

Sanae jumped up and ran off in pursuit of the wheelchair.

'Kinoshita? Why would Kinoshita be here? He's supposed to be in the hospital—.'

Kyōzō was still stunned, but Shinji tapped his brother on the shoulder.

'Quick! Up ahead is—.'

Kyōzō immediately realised what Shinji was trying to tell him, and flew out of the shop.

The wheelchair had picked up speed, and was moving down the slope at the same speed as Sanae could run in her pumps.

'Inspector! Quickly!'

Kinoshita turned white.

There was a concrete staircase up ahead.

The nickname the regulars of Sunny Side Up—the female students of P Academy—had given to the two-hundred-step-long staircase was the Heart Killer.

Sanae tried to run even harder, but her pumps came loose and she tripped.

Because Shinji and Kyōzō had to run around her, they missed grabbing the wheelchair by a hair's breadth.

Kinoshita and the wheelchair suddenly disappeared from their sight, but were followed by the noise of metal hitting concrete. After one especially loud bang, it all went silent.

Should they call an ambulance, or an undertaker?

'Sanae hates you too!'

A weak voice, more a dark curse than anything, reached their ears.

Finally, something that guy is good at, thought Kyōzō.

Kinoshita was obviously immortal. He might be well suited to be a police detective after all.

NOTES

[i] TRANSLATOR'S NOTE: The main building of the Tōkyō Metropolitan Police Department is located near Sakuradamon, one of the gates of ancient Edo Castle. The current Imperial Palace is built on the site of Edo Castle. The term Sakuradamon is often used as slang among police officers to indicate the MPD headquarters.

[ii] AUTHOR'S NOTE: *The Border-Line Case* (1936) by Margery Allingham. A police officer discovers a dead body on the border of his own jurisdiction and moves the body so the case would go to another police officer, and inadvertently makes it appear like an impossible crime. Not clear whether this work was meant to be a serious work, or a work of comedy.

[iii] Hachikō (1923-1935) was an Akita dog who is remembered for his extraordinary loyalty to his owner. His master Professor Hidesaburō Ueno commuted every day to his university, and at the end of each day Hachikō would leave their house to pick his master up from Shibuya Station. One day, Ueno suffered a cerebral haemorrhage during a lecture, and died without ever returning. For the next nine years, Hachikō would go every day to Shibuya Station at the time the train arrived, awaiting the return of his master. A bronze statue of Hachikō has been erected in front of Shibuya Station.

[iv] TRANSLATOR'S NOTE: *Kōjō no Tsuki, or The Moon Over the Ruined Castle*, is a song written in 1901 by Rentarō Taki, originally intended as a music lesson song for high school students.

[v] TRANSLATOR'S NOTE: It is custom in Japan not to wear shoes inside the house. Slippers are used instead, and guests are always offered slippers to wear.

[vi] AUTHOR'S NOTE: *The Big Bow Mystery* (1891) by Israel Zangwill. Considered to be the first locked room mystery that involves deception about the time of the crime. For present-day readers, the story might not feel fresh anymore as the main trick has

been reused repeatedly by various writers ever since, but it remains a pioneering masterpiece.

[vii] AUTHOR'S NOTE: *The Emperor's Snuff-Box* (1942) by John Dickson Carr. This novel was widely praised by Agatha Christie, and is quite unlike most other works by Carr. Although a very well-written novel, it is less well-regarded by Carr fans.

[viii] AUTHOR'S NOTE: By far the best-known fictional detective created by John Dickson Carr. It is said Dr. Fell is based on fellow detective author G.K. Chesterton.

[ix] AUTHOR'S NOTE: Full name: Sir Henry Merrivale. Like Dr. Fell, H.M is a detective created by John Dickson Carr, but H.M. appears in the novels published under the name Carter Dickson. He is allegedly based on Churchill. The H.M. novels tend to feel less refined in comparison to those featuring Dr. Fell.

[x] AUTHOR'S NOTE: Dr. Dermot Kinross is a psychologist, who only appears in *The Emperor's Snuff-Box*. Carr created other great detectives who only appeared in one novel, like Dr. John Gaunt, Gordon Cross and others.

[xi] AUTHOR'S NOTE: A fictional detective created by F.W. Crofts. The quintessential example of the police detective who solves his cases by old-fashioned footwork.

[xii] TRANSLATOR'S NOTE: Yuming is the nickname of the Japanese singer Yumi Matsutoya. She is one of the iconic figures in the world of Japanese pop music, with more than 42 million records sold.

[xiii] AUTHOR'S NOTE: An expression often uttered by Dr. Fell, not H.M. But I'm sure nobody will realise that unless they go through the trouble of checking it out for themselves.

[xiv] AUTHOR'S NOTE: The famous words Archimedes cried before he became the world's first streaker. For the younger readers among us: streaking basically means running around town completely naked.

It was popular all around the world about thirty years ago. In Japan it is, of course, in violation of public indecency regulations.

[xv] TRANSLATOR'S NOTE: Mori-no-Ishimatsu was the number one henchman of the chivalrous yakuza gangster and gambler Shimizu-no-Jirochō who lived in the mid-nineteenth century Japan. Both his master and Ishimatsu himself have been immortalised as folk heroes on film and television drama adapating their adventures. In Torazō Hirosawa (1899-1964)'s narrative song *Ishimatsu on the 30-koku Ferry Boat*, a man from Edo (Tōkyō) travelling on a ferry is treated to copious amounts of sushi and sake for his praise for yakuza and the gang of Shimizu-no-Jirochō in particular, not realising his conversation partner is in fact Mori-no-Ishimatsu.

[xvi] AUTHOR'S NOTE: *The Hollow Man* (1935), published in the United States as *The Three Coffins*, by John Dickson Carr. The Japanese translation follows the US title. Many consider this the best work by Carr, but there are also many people who are very critical of the novel, possibly because it features a physical trick that is not very convincing at an instinctive level. However, even if one ignores the locked room lecture and the tricks played out, this novel offers interesting play with double meanings and an excellent structure, making it one of the most outstanding works of the entire Golden Age of detective fiction.

[xvii] TRANSLATOR'S NOTE: Edogawa Rampo (1894-1964. Real name: Tarō Hirai) was a prominent Japanese mystery author and critic, often considered to be the father of Japanese mystery fiction. The pseudonym Edogawa Rampo is based phonetically on Edgar Allen Poe. The essay *A Classification of Tricks* (*Ruibetsu Torikku Shūsei*, 1953) is a comprehensive classification of all tricks utilised in mystery fiction, going beyond only locked room mysteries.

[xviii] AUTHOR'S NOTE: One of the stories collected in *The Case-Book of Sherlock Holmes*. A woman is found dead on a bridge, her head shot from close distance. The weapon is not found. Another woman is suspected of the murder, but she denies it. As to how it was done, a rock had been tied to the revolver with a rope, and the rope had been

suspended over the side of the bridge. After the victim committed suicide, the rock pulled the revolver into the river below.

[xix] TRANSLATOR'S NOTE: Jirō Akagawa (born 1948) is a Japanese mystery novelist who was especially prolific in the late 70s until the late 80s. Two of his best known series are *Three Sisters Investigate* (*Sanshimai Tantei Dan*) and *Tortoiseshell Cat Holmes* (*Mikeneko Hōmuzu*), both well over twenty volumes each. *The Deduction of Tortoiseshell Cat Holmes* (*Mikeneko Hōmuzu no Suiri*), published in 1978, is the first novel in the *Tortoiseshell Cat Holmes* series.

[xx] AUTHOR'S NOTE: *The Curse of the Bronze Lamp* (1945) by Carter Dickson. One of Sherlock Holmes' unrecorded stories, about the disappearance of Mr. Filmore, serves as the basis of the plot. It happens often, not only with Carr, that a story starts out promising only to falter in the end, and this novel is no exception.

[xxi] AUTHOR'S NOTE: *Death from a Top Hat* (1938) by Clayton Rawson. Rawson performed stage magic under the name The Great Merlini, and he used that name for his fictional detective, similar to our own magician-mystery author Tsumao Awasaka. Rawson has something to say about Carr's locked room lecture in *Death from a Top Hat*.

[xxii] AUTHOR'S NOTE: *Off the Face of the Earth* (1947) by Clayton Rawson. A person tailed by two police detectives steps inside one of a row of telephone booths and disappears from it. The Great Merlini realises how it was done, and re-enacts the disappearance act under different circumstances.

[xxiii] TRANSLATOR'S NOTE: *Sabu* was a gay men's magazine published between 1974 and 2002. It was one of the earliest publications for gay men in Japan.

[xxiv] AUTHOR'S NOTE: *The Nine Mile Walk* (1947) by Harry Kemelman. A short story included in a short story collection with the same title.

[xxv] TRANSLATOR'S NOTE: The Rokumeikan, or Deer-Cry Pavilion, was a large building constructed in 1883 in Tōkyō. It was used to accommodate and entertain foreign guests of the government, and became a symbol of Westernisation because of the many parties and balls following Western manners held there. It was demolished in 1941.